Camp
Carter
by

Kathi Daley

Chapter 1

Wednesday May 24

The fact that Zak had signed us up to act as chaperones for Scooter's end-of-school-year campout was bad enough. The fact that there wasn't a bathroom in sight of the cabin Zak and I had been assigned was even worse. But the fact that I was six weeks pregnant and dealing with relentless bouts of morning sickness almost had me running back home to my hometown of Ashton Falls with my tail between my legs.

"What am I going to do?" I asked my best friend, Ellie Denton, who had stayed behind with her husband, Levi, new baby Eli, and our resident animals. "I'm never going to survive without a bathroom." I walked farther into the forest as I tried to find the sweet spot where cell reception would be the strongest. It seemed that every time I found a strong signal the reception faded and I needed to seek out the next best location to have this very important conversation.

"What you're going to do is tell your very sweet and very caring husband that you're going to have his baby. Not only is there no way you'll be able to continue to hide your condition while camping in that tiny cabin but there's absolutely no reason for you to do so."

"You know what happened last time. You know why I wanted to wait."

Ellie paused and took a deep breath. I was sure she was trying to channel the patience she knew she'd need to deal with my irrational emotions. Yes, I'd experienced a setback at Christmas, when it turned out that my first pregnancy didn't take, but even I had to admit I'd been a handful as of late. I cried when I was happy, I cried when I was sad, I cried just because, but the one thing I never let myself do was cry in front of Zak. At least he'd been busy with the remodel of the boathouse and the end-of-year activities at Zimmerman Academy, which had just let out for the summer the previous Friday. So far, I don't think he'd had the time to really notice my crazy mood swings.

"Zoe, you know I love you and you know I only want what's best for you, but you have to tell him. You should have already. The longer you wait the more awkward it's going to be. Besides, while he hasn't said as much, I'm willing to bet he already knows."

"I've been careful."

"He loves you. He's in tune with your moods. He seems to be aware of everything that's going on with you. He always has been."

I sat down on a rock overlooking the warm shallow lake. "Then why hasn't he said anything?"

Ellie sighed. "Honestly? I think he wants to give you the time and space you need to work through your issues. Zak really is the most patient man on the planet."

Ellie was right. Zak was very patient and he probably did already know or at least suspect I was pregnant. And he probably *had* decided to give me the space I needed to deal with whatever it was I was so worried about. Zac was a saint; he'd proven on more than one occasion that he was willing to let me set the pace in our relationship.

"Okay," I finally said. "I'll tell him." I put my hand to my churning stomach. "He's hiking with Scooter, Alex, Charlie, and some of the counselors, but as soon as he gets back, I'll tell him."

"Good. I'm glad. He's going to be so happy."

I smiled. "Yeah. He will."

"You're going to be a mom!" Ellie said, a squeal of happiness in her voice. "We're going to be moms together. I've been dying for you to tell Zak so I can finally tell Levi."

"I'll call you after I talk to Zak, but don't tell Levi before I do. The guy is a real blabbermouth."

"Don't worry; I won't say a word until you give me the green light."

After I hung up with Ellie I made what I would later look back on as a huge mistake. The thought of finally telling Zak my secret was making me more nauseated than I already was, so I headed over to the rustic kitchen to ask the cook for a few saltine crackers and some club soda. Camp Carter was a wilderness camp about sixty miles from Ashton Falls. It was nestled in the foothills of the mountains I call home, so the midspring temperatures were already climbing into the high seventies in the lower elevations, while the high temperatures back home on the mountain still lingered in the low sixties. The lake the camp was built beside was warm and shallow, perfect for swimming and canoeing even early in the season.

Zak and I, along with my dog Charlie and the two twelve-year-olds who lived with us, Scooter Sherwood and Alex Bremmerton, had arrived early to help get things up and running. By the time the sun set over the distant mountain the camp would be filled with more than a hundred students from four elementary schools who would spend five fun-filled days under the constant care of ten camp counselors, two activities leaders, a cook, an administrator, and a handful of selfless parents who'd agreed to act as chaperones.

At the moment there were six counselors on the premises, in addition to the cook and the camp administrator. The rest of the staff and the campers would be arriving on the buses the administrator had hired later that afternoon. It was a warm spring day and everyone who'd arrived early had decided to go hiking. I had chosen to rest instead of recreate and was fairly sure I was the only one, other than the cook, left in the area where the cabins and other buildings were located.

"Mrs. Potter," I called as I walked through the dirty screen door. "It's Zoe Zimmerman. Are you here?" I scratched at a mosquito bite that had shown up on my thigh just below the hem of my shorts as I walked farther into the room.

I looked around and didn't see the cook, although there was a pot of gray goop I assumed must be some sort of gravy simmering on the stove. I put my hand over my mouth and looked away, fighting the nausea that had suddenly intensified. If I didn't find something to calm the rumbling in my stomach I was afraid I was going to be the architect of a huge mess all over the kitchen floor.

Given the fact that the room was empty, I had to assume Mrs. Potter had stepped out. I really needed something to calm my stomach, so I figured I'd look for the crackers myself. I opened several cupboards filled with canned goods, paper products, seasonings, and pots and pans, but nothing resembling a cracker. I was about to give up when I noticed a doorway on the far end of the long kitchen that either led outdoors or, more probably, to a pantry or storage room. I tried opening the door, but something had fallen behind it and it wouldn't budge. I leaned my hip into it and pushed, getting the door to open a tiny bit. Most people wouldn't have been able to squeeze through the small opening, but it just so happens I'm smaller than most, so I was able to push my way through. I had to suck in my gut as I tried to maneuver in the tight space, but after a fair amount of effort I found myself propelled into the space behind the door. I turned to see what had blocked it, and that was when I finally lost the lunch I'd been trying so desperately to hang on to.

******

"I'm going to need you to come down to the station," the tall man in the blue police uniform who showed up after just a couple of minutes and introduced himself as Officer Michaelson informed me. "Officer Williams will escort you. When you arrive at the station, Detective Swanson will take your statement."

I looked down at the blood on my hands and nodded. As soon as I'd realized Mrs. Potter had very recently been stabbed and was at that point still alive, I'd tried to stop the bleeding, but it had all been for naught. Still, in the course of removing the knife and trying to slow the flow of blood, I'd managed to get my fingerprints on the murder weapon and

Mrs. Potter's blood on my hands and clothing.

"My husband is hiking," I informed him. "Can someone find him and tell him what's happened? He'll worry if he gets back and I'm not here."

"We'll locate him and let him know what's happened."

I felt as if I was in a trance as Officer Williams led me to his car. He helped me into the backseat, but at least he didn't cuff me. For reasons even I couldn't explain, it seemed everyone other than me had gone off in one direction or another, so I was the only one on the premises to try to explain how I had ended up holding the murder weapon but definitely hadn't been the one to wield it. I suppose it would have been better if I'd been the one to call in the murder, but that wasn't what had happened; Officer Michaelson had shown up before I'd even gotten through to 911. I guess Mrs. Potter had known she was in trouble and had called herself before hiding in the pantry. It was obvious to me the killer had found her and stuck a knife in her chest before escaping through the partially open window. But all Officer Michaelson found when he arrived was me standing over her body with the bloody knife in my hand and a look of shock on my face.

The ride into the small town of Duck Lake was a silent one. I sat nervously in the backseat trying to figure out exactly how I'd gotten myself into my current situation while the policeman in the front seat focused on the road ahead of him. So far, I hadn't been arrested, but I had the feeling if I didn't come up with a reasonable explanation for the scene he'd found when he'd arrived an official arrest might be the next thing in my future.

When I arrived at the Duck Lake Police Station it was explained to me that my clothing was evidence because it was covered with Mrs. Potter's blood. Officer Williams took swabs of the blood on my hands before handing me a jumpsuit to change into so my clothing could be logged in.

I felt numb as I went through the motions of changing my clothes and washing as much blood as I could from my skin. Then I was led into an interrogation room, where I was offered a glass of water and told to wait. I looked at my reflection in the two-way mirror while I waited for Detective Swanson to join me. Yikes. I really looked a fright. No wonder the cops thought I was guilty. Despite the fact that

I'd already washed up I looked like I'd just survived hand-to-hand combat.

"Ms. Zimmerman?" A short man with graying hair and faded blue eyes greeted me.

"Yes. I'm Zoe Zimmerman."

"My name is Detective Swanson. I'll be taking your statement. I need you to state your full name for the record."

"Zoe Harlow Donovan Zimmerman. Am I under arrest?"

"Not at this point. I do, however, have some questions I need you to answer. It's important that you answer as completely and honestly as possible."

I nodded. "Okay. I have nothing to hide. Ask away."

"Why were you at the camp today?"

"My husband, Zak Zimmerman, volunteered the two of us to be parent chaperones for the sixth-grade trip the camp is hosting. Our son…well, I guess technically he isn't our son, but we love him like he is, is in the sixth grade at Ashton Falls Elementary, so he was invited." I knew I was rambling, but all I could think of was telling the detective everything so he wouldn't get the idea I was holding anything back or lying.

"When we arrived the only people on the premises seemed to be you and Mrs. Potter," Detective Swanson stated.

"Most of the kids and staff are arriving later this afternoon. Zak and I, along with the two minors who live with us, Scooter Sherwood and Alex Bremmerton, arrived early to help get things set up. After we got everything ready the others decided to go for a hike. I wasn't feeling well, so I stayed behind. I believe Mrs. Potter stayed behind to get the evening meal ready for the campers when they showed up."

He sat back in his chair and studied me as I spoke. The entire situation had left me feeling vulnerable and scared.

"And who else arrived early besides yourself and your family?"

"Gina Keebler, the camp administrator, was already on site when we arrived, as was Mrs. Potter. And six counselors showed up early. I don't know their last names, but their first names are Seth, Felix, Darrell, Gordy, Susan, and Polly. There was also a man named Bryson Young and his son Peter. Like Zak and me, Bryson is a parent volunteer."

"Was there anyone else on the premises?"

"There was a man. A janitor or maintenance man of some sort. I didn't speak to him, but I think I overheard Gina say his name was Fred. Again, I don't know his last name. I'm sure Gina can give you that information."

Detective Swanson jotted down a few notes before asking his next question. "I need you to describe to me everything that happened from the time you arrived at the camp until the time the police showed up."

I took a sip of my water. "Okay. I'll do my best." I took a deep breath and tried to calm my nerves. "Let's see. Zak and I, along with the other members of the camp staff who had arrived early, were shown to our cabins and then asked to assemble in the cafeteria. I guess that was around nine o'clock this morning. Gina gave us an overview of what we could expect from the long weekend, as well as a list of tasks we would be asked to orchestrate. Once the introductions were made and the orientation was over, everyone was assigned our chores to do before the campers arrived this afternoon."

"Chores?"

"Things like stocking the activities room, opening up the cabins, shelving supplies. We were each given different tasks. When they were done everyone decided to take a hike while we waited for the larger group to arrive. I wasn't feeling well, so I went back to my cabin to lie down."

"Did you notice tension between Mrs. Potter and anyone else this morning?"

I shook my head. "Mrs. Potter was only with us for a few minutes. Gina introduced her and then she went back to the kitchen. I guess she had quite a bit to do to get everything ready. This is the first group of campers this season, so she needed to completely stock the kitchen."

"During the course of the day did you notice anyone hanging out in or around the kitchen?"

"I didn't notice, but to be honest, I wasn't paying all that much attention."

The detective paused when Officer Williams came in, whispered something in his ear, and left again. The detective turned his attention back to me. "Okay; walk me through exactly what occurred after you went to your cabin to lay down."

"I took a short nap and everyone was still gone when I woke up. I called my best friend, Ellie Denton, and chatted with her for a while, and then I went to the kitchen to see if I could get some crackers to calm my stomach. When I got there I thought the place was deserted and Mrs. Potter had stepped out. I couldn't find the crackers in the cupboards, so I tried the pantry. The door was blocked, but I managed to get it open far enough so I could squeeze in. As soon as I did, I realized the reason the door was blocked was because Mrs. Potter way laying in front of it."

"And what did you do at that point?"

"I ran over to her and knelt down beside her. She was unconscious but had a weak pulse. I found some dish towels and applied pressure to the area around the stab wound. She was bleeding so much. I couldn't get it to stop. After a minute, I realized her heart had stopped beating. I tried to call 911 for help, but there was no reception in the pantry. The cell service on the campgrounds is sketchy. I wanted to try CPR, but the knife was still in her chest. I pulled it out and was looking for a place to put it when Officer Michaelson showed up."

"So Officer Michaelson busted through the door and you were standing over the body with the murder weapon in your hand."

"I was kneeling over the body, not standing, but yes, that's the gist of it."

"Did it occur to you that it might be a bad idea to remove the knife in the first place?"

"It did, which is why I didn't remove it right away. But once her heart stopped I didn't know what else to do. There was no way I could perform CPR with the knife still stuck in her chest and I had no reason to believe the police would arrive so quickly. How *did* Officer Michaelson show up so fast?"

"He was in the area on another call when the 911 call came through."

"Oh. I guess that makes sense. Anyway, I know it looks bad that I was holding the murder weapon, but you have to believe I would never hurt Mrs. Potter— or anyone for that matter."

There was a pause as the door opened and Officer Williams brought in a folder. He handed it to Detective Swanson and left the room. Swanson opened the folder and considered the contents before looking up and speaking. "It says here you often assist the sheriff in Ashton Falls with murder investigations."

"Yes. Sheriff Salinger. You can call him. I'm sure he'll vouch for me."

"Someone is on the phone with him as we speak. I also understand you and your husband run a private school for gifted children."

I nodded. "Phyllis King is our school administrator. She'll vouch for me also." I took a deep breath. "I'm a nice person. Really. I would never hurt anyone."

He looked down at the file again. "It says here that you're pregnant."

I frowned. "I am, but how did you know that?"

"I have a statement from your husband, who's being interviewed in the next room. He's verified almost everything you've told me, although you haven't mentioned the pregnancy yet—which, I assume, is why you were looking for the crackers."

I closed my eyes and let out a groan. "I haven't told anyone yet. Not even Zak."

"Well, apparently he figured it out. It says here you're about six weeks along. According to Officer Michaelson, who's interviewing your husband, he's very concerned that you not be caused any undue stress, given your situation."

I ran my hands through my thick, curly hair. Suddenly I felt the urge to throw up again.

"Would you say you're experiencing undue stress?" the detective asked.

I took a sip of water and looked back at the detective, whose eyes were pinned on me with a hard stare. "I'll admit this whole thing has been very upsetting and I'm sure it's affected both my stress level and my blood pressure, but I'm certain the baby and I are fine right now at least. I'd love to get out of here, though. Am I under arrest or am I going to be allowed to go?"

The detective continued to glance through the folder without answering. Finally, he closed it and looked at me. "You're free to go; however, we'll need you to be available for further questions. I understand you'll be at the camp through Monday."

I narrowed my gaze. "I guess. Are they still going to hold the camp?"

"Yes. The kids arrived shortly after you were brought in."

"Do you think the kids are in any danger?"

"We have no reason to believe the person who stabbed Mrs. Potter poses a threat to anyone else. In most cases a murder like this is personal, directed toward the victim and the victim alone. If additional information indicates otherwise we would, of course, evacuate the camp. The kitchen has been closed temporarily, however, and a uniformed officer has been assigned to keep an eye on things."

"They closed the kitchen? There are more than a hundred people to feed."

"Boxed meals are being sent to the camp until we can complete our investigation and reopen the facility. Before you leave I want you to think carefully about the movements of the people at the camp this morning. Is there anyone you feel stands out as more of a suspect than anyone else?"

I thought about each person individually. Gina Keebler was a single woman in her midthirties who, I understand, had worked at the camp for more than a decade. She appeared to be friendly and energetic and genuinely thrilled that the camp was opening for the season. I remembered someone saying Mrs. Potter had worked for the camp for almost as long, so it stood to reason the two women would be friends, although I supposed because they had the longest history with the camp and each other, they had the greatest potential to have grievances against each other as well.

All the counselors who'd arrived early had been with the camp for at least one previous season. I seemed to remember Seth had been there the longest, with six summers under his belt. He was friendly and appeared to be in his late thirties or early forties, older by a decade than any of the other counselors. He seemed to be the second in command behind Gina.

The youngest of the returning counselors was Polly. She was twenty-one and was returning for her second year as a counselor at Camp Carter. She was fun and friendly and I couldn't see her putting a knife in anyone's chest. It seemed like she and Gordy might have a thing going on. Gordy was probably in his late twenties and had been with the camp for the past four summers. While I didn't think they were openly a couple, I'd seen them smiling at each other throughout the orientation, and there was a certain awareness and tension between them that couldn't be ignored. The thing I found most intriguing about their exchanges was that Polly had a huge diamond ring on her left hand, which seemed to indicate she was engaged, though I got the distinct feeling it wasn't Gordy she was engaged to.

Felix seemed to be the most stoic of the group. If I had to guess I'd say he was probably around thirty. The thing that was most noteworthy about him was that he presented a serious demeanor that at times seemed overly harsh. He asked a lot of questions about rules and regulations, and although we'd been in the same room for several hours, I'd never seen him smile. I remembered thinking he didn't seem to have the right personality for a counselor at a kids' camp, but I hadn't seen him in action, so perhaps he'd loosen up when the kids were here.

And then there was Darrell. He appeared to be in his midtwenties and was almost as big a goofball as my Scooter. I wondered if he would be able to keep his group on task and out of trouble or if he might play the role of instigator to any trouble his campers got into.

Susan was at the camp for her third year. She seemed to be most focused on the programs and activities that would be offered this year and appeared to have a lot of ideas she wanted to see implemented. If anything, she was almost too enthusiastic, often interrupting the flow of the orientation to offer her own ideas and suggestions. I could sense a tension between her and Gina, which I supposed I could understand because it appeared Susan was interested in running the whole show.

As I'd already told the detective, I hadn't spoken to Fred, the maintenance man, so I didn't have an opinion as to the likelihood of him having a grudge against Mrs. Potter. The only other adult at the meeting that morning, in addition to Zak and me, was Peter's father, Bryson Young, who had listened intently but hadn't said much.

"No," I finally said. "No one I've met stands out over anyone else."

"Okay. Then you're free to go. We'll be in touch to follow up in a day or two."

I took a deep breath as I stood up. I turned and walked to the door. I'd managed to get through my interrogation unscathed, but now I had to face Zak, who apparently knew I'd been keeping my pregnancy from him all along.

When I entered the waiting area he was pacing back and forth. When he saw me, he opened his arms, which for some reason made me immediately start to sob. He hurried over to where I was standing and wrapped me in his arms. He didn't say anything, but I knew at once that he wasn't mad I'd tried to keep my pregnancy from him and did, in fact, love me despite the irrational behavior I seemed prone to.

Chapter 2

"I'm sorry I didn't tell you sooner," I said to Zak as soon as we'd left the police station and were walking to the car in the parking lot. His large hand enveloped mine and I found I felt both safe and vulnerable. "I wanted to, but I was afraid to believe it was real after what happened the last time."

Zak stopped walking, turned, and faced me. He put a hand on my cheek and looked into my eyes. "It's okay. I understand. I knew you would tell me when you were ready and I was fine with waiting."

"You aren't mad?"

Zak leaned forward and kissed me gently on the lips. "I'm not mad. In fact, I'm ecstatically happy."

I smiled. "Yeah."

Zak pulled me into his large chest and wrapped his arms around me. I could feel the emotion in the strength of his arms as they held me close, as if he'd never let me go. After a minute he loosened his grip and took a step back. He took my hand and we continued toward the car. "I'll admit I envisioned an entirely different setting from a police station parking lot when you finally did tell me."

I shrugged. "You know me; I like to keep things interesting. Besides, I seem to attract trouble, and pregnancy apparently hasn't changed that. I've been thinking about the murder and I can't for the life of me figure out who might have done it. I don't suppose you saw or overheard anything when you were out hiking today?"

Zak opened the door for me and I slipped onto the passenger seat. He walked around the car and got in through the driver's door before he answered. "I assume you plan to investigate."

"I'm not sure, though I suppose I might ask around."

"Asking around is investigating and it could be dangerous."

"I'm the only suspect at this point," I reminded Zak. "Sure, they let me go for now, but that doesn't mean they aren't planning to try to build a case against me. Was anyone from the orientation this morning not with you on the hike?"

Zak started the car and pulled onto the street. He turned onto the highway before he answered. "Actually, there were only a few of us on the hike. Alex, Scooter, Charlie, and I joined Bryson, Peter, and another mother and son who showed up just before we left: Jackie Warlap and her son Bobby.

"I thought the counselors were going with you."

"I did too. Initially, Gina showed up at the meeting place along with Seth and Darrell. We were chatting about the best hike to take when Susan showed up and announced there was a problem that needed Gina's attention. Gina left with her and shortly after that Seth decided he had something to do as well. Polly and Gordy never did show up, but it seemed to me that they were just waiting for an opportunity to be alone together."

"I had that same impression," I said. "Although, it looked to me based on the rock on her finger that Polly's engaged, and it seems Gordy isn't the guy she's engaged to."

Zak frowned. "Yeah, I had that same thought. Still, a cheating fiancée doesn't necessarily equate to a killer."

"True. So what about Felix? Did he ever show up?"

"He made an appearance just as we were setting out, but it didn't take long for Darrell and him to get into an argument. We'd only hiked about a half mile before Darrell got fed up with his nagging and made an excuse to leave. Felix stayed with us for another fifteen minutes or so and then made his own excuse to head back."

"So if none of the counselors were with you by the time I found Mrs. Potter in the pantry, where were they? I didn't see a sign of anyone when I left the cabin looking for some crackers after I called Ellie."

Zak narrowed his gaze. "I don't know, but I suppose it would be prudent for us to find out. It seems the only adults who couldn't have killed Mrs. Potter are me, Bryson, and Ginny."

"And me," I added.

Zak smiled. "Of course. That goes without saying."

The conversation stalled as we pulled onto the camp road. The scene at the facility was a lot different than it had been when I'd been driven away. For one thing, there were sixth graders everywhere. Talk about a general atmosphere of chaos.

"Let's not mention the baby to the kids just yet," I said to Zak.

"Alex already knows."

I raised a brow. "She does? Since when?"

"Since before I knew. I figured it out when we were on Maui, but when we got home you were so sick. Alex was concerned and came to talk to me. She said she'd suspected you might be pregnant at Easter but figured it wasn't her place to say anything."

I rolled my eyes. "Geez. Me and my big secret. My mom figured it out, Ellie figured it out, Alex figured it out, and you figured it out. Is there anyone who *doesn't* know?"

"I'm pretty sure Scooter doesn't suspect a thing, but I've noticed Levi frowning at you whenever you announce you're exhausted and going to bed and it isn't even nine o'clock yet."

Zak had a point. Even though I hadn't been admitting I was pregnant, I'd been acting as if I were. It was no wonder people had figured it out. My dad probably knew as well and most likely so did Jeremy Fisher, the manager of the wild and domestic animal rescue and rehabilitation shelter I owned, who had a child of his own and knew the signs to look for.

I glanced down at the jumpsuit I was still wearing. "I don't want anyone to see me wearing this. Do you think maybe you can skirt around the back using the maintenance road and get me as close to the cabin as possible?" I looked at the blood still evident on my arms and hands. "And I could use a shower too."

"I don't think anyone has noticed us so far. I'll park the car on the road and sneak back to get you some clothes," Zak said. "I'll take you into town and we can rent a room at that little place by the river. You can take a shower, get changed, and then we'll grab a bite to eat before we head back to the camp."

"The kids will be worried."

"Call Alex to let her know what we're doing. She can fill Scooter in. I'm sure once you assure her that you're fine she'll be fine. There are a ton of kids here her age to keep her occupied."

"Okay. And we can return this one-piece monstrosity while we're at it."

Zak leaned over and gave me a quick kiss on the lips. "Hang tight. I'll hurry."

I called and spoke to Alex while I waited for Zak. I assured her that I was fine and filled her in on Zak's plan. I could sense she was worried, but she said she'd be fine until we returned and she'd even keep an eye on Scooter and Charlie. I used to think it was ridiculous that Alex felt the need to watch out for Scooter, who was the same age she was, but I'd learned with time that Alex might be twelve in years, but she was at least thirty in terms of intelligence and maturity.

Zak was true to his word, returning to the truck with a small bag filled with clothes and toiletries almost before I'd finished my call with Alex. When we arrived at the motel I took a long, hot shower, attempting to erase all evidence of the afternoon's ordeal from my body. As I washed my hair for the third time, I closed my eyes and tried to eradicate the image of Mrs. Potter lying in a pool of her own blood from my mind. I hoped she'd find peace in the afterlife and I prayed for her family, but I knew I wouldn't find my own sense of serenity until I identified and brought to justice the person who had ended her life.

By the time I finished my shower and had dressed in clean clothes Zak had picked up takeout and set it up on the small table in front of the window. I wasn't hungry, but it had been hours since I'd eaten and I needed to remember I wasn't only eating for myself but for my baby as well.

"I wasn't sure what you'd want, so I got a little of everything," Zak said.

It looked like he had enough food to feed not just us but everyone we'd left behind at the camp too, but Zak being thorough was just him being Zak. I chose a turkey sandwich on whole grain bread and a small fruit salad. He handed me a bottle of water, which was about the only thing I was drinking these days.

I took several bites of the sandwich, then leaned back to digest a bit before I continued. I'd learned since I'd been pregnant that it was important to eat slowly if I wanted to keep what I ate on the inside.

"How are you feeling?" Zak asked, concern evident on his face.

"I'm fine, just a bit shell-shocked now that everything is sinking in." I felt a tear slide down my cheek. "I can't imagine why anyone would do something so horrible to another person."

Zak put his hand over mine and gave it a little squeeze. I'd investigated a lot of murders and each one was horrific in its own way. This one was certainly no worse than the others; maybe it was the pregnancy hormones making me overly emotional.

"And the baby?" Zak asked.

I put a hand on my stomach, which was just beginning to develop a tiny bump that wasn't recognizable yet. "She's fine."

"She?" Zak asked.

"It's too early to know for sure, but I know it's a she. Catherine."

Recognition dawned on Zak's face. "From the castle in Ireland."

"On that last day at the castle Catherine the ghost told me I was going to have a little girl of my own named Catherine. Now, she didn't specify that Catherine would be my first child, but somehow I know the baby I'm carrying is the baby Lady Catherine spoke of. I hope that's okay. Were you hoping for a boy?"

Zak placed both his hands over mine, smiled, and looked deeply into my eyes. "I think a little girl named after her great, great, great, however many greats grandmother is just about perfect."

I felt a sense of peace fill my heart. I'd met Catherine when Zak and I had visited a haunted castle in Ireland a couple of years back. The most amazing thing was that I'd learned while we were there that a previous lady of the castle might have been my ancestor generations back. I didn't have proof of that at the time, but I was intrigued enough to hire a private investigator to help me find out. After almost two years he'd proven to an 80 percent accuracy that Catherine Dunphy, wife of Lord Carrick Dunphy and mother of twelve children, really was the mother of my first Donovan ancestor, who, as it turned out, was a Dunphy by blood, not a Donovan. Of course, I didn't really need the proof I'd sought; the minute I met Catherine's ghost I knew in my heart we were linked by blood, a shared history, and an intertwined destiny.

"We should find an opportunity to tell Scooter about the baby," I said as I nibbled a few bites of fruit. "I don't want him to feel left out in any way."

"When we get back to the camp we'll pull both Scooter and Alex aside and fill them in on everything that's going on. I bet both kids are going to be thrilled to have a baby in the house."

"I hope so. It's occurred to me that bringing a biological child into the mix might make them feel slighted somehow."

"They know we love them as if they're our real children and if they begin to feel insecure we'll remind them of that. I'm afraid the child who may deal with a bit of jealousy is Charlie."

Zak had a point. Charlie had been my sidekick since before I started dating Zak, way before Alex and Scooter came into my life. "If Charlie is jealous of Catherine I'll just need to be sure he understands I don't love him any less even though I have another baby in my life. Besides, he adores Eli."

"That's true. Maybe he'll be fine."

I really hoped so. Charlie was so sweet and not at all the jealous sort, but having Ellie's baby in the house wasn't the same as having a baby I'd be holding a lot of the time.

"We should get back to the camp," I said after a bit.

"You didn't eat more than a few bites."

"I know, but I'm not really hungry. Maybe we can sneak all this back to our cabin in case I wake up in the middle of the night with the munchies. I have a feeling I'm not going to want to go searching in the kitchen again for something to snack on."

"We'll stop by that little market on the corner and grab some snacks and an ice cooler. That way we'll have whatever we need without having to go to the kitchen."

"And water," I added. "I've been drinking a lot of bottled water."

At the minimarket Zak went in search of a cooler and some ice while I filled a basket with everything chocolate. I wasn't sure where the craving had come from, but suddenly I found myself almost willing to sacrifice a limb for chocolate cookies, doughnuts, and candy bars. I hoped this craving for chocolate didn't last my entire pregnancy or I was going to look like a whale before I gave birth, but I'd had a hard day, so I'd decided that for now at least, if Catherine wanted chocolate cupcakes Catherine should have chocolate cupcakes.

When we arrived at the camp Zak went in search of Alex, Scooter, and Charlie, while I called Ellie to let her know the cat was out of the bag and it was fine to confirm to Levi what he most likely already suspected. Then I called my mom and told her I'd finally told Zak and it was fine to tell my dad, to which she'd replied that he'd figured it out a long time ago. It amazed me that while so many people apparently knew my big secret the only two to confront me with it were Ellie and my mother. I owed thanks to a lot of people for respecting my wishes and giving me the space I needed.

Alex hugged me the minute she walked into the cabin with Scooter, Charlie, and Zak on her heels. "Are you okay? I was so scared when they told me that they took you to jail."

"I'm fine. I told you that on the phone. You seemed fine."

"I was scared to death but being brave. Scooter too."

I glanced over Alex's head at Scooter, who was standing behind her looking uncertain. I opened my arms and invited him in. Once I'd reassured both kids that I was perfectly okay I asked them to sit down, gave them each one of my doughnuts, and told them we'd be welcoming a new member of the family into our home just after the first of the year.

******

We answered all the kids' questions, then got them settled into the cabins they'd been assigned to with their peers and Zak and I sat down to map out a strategy for the investigation we'd only have a few days to complete. He logged onto his computer using the hot spot from his satellite phone, which had a lot better reception than my cell, while I grabbed a yellow legal pad and a pen from his bag.

"Unless there was someone on the property we don't know about there are only eight suspects," I began. I said the names aloud as I jotted them down in a row on the pad. "Gina, Seth, Polly, Gordy, Felix, Darrell, Susan, and the janitor, whose name, I think, is Fred. All of them have spent one or more summers at the camp, so all of them knew Mrs. Potter. I haven't picked up vibes of any sort regarding who may have had a reason to kill her."

"I agree," Zak said. "It's most likely one of the eight people you've listed will turn out to be the killer. The best plan of attack is probably speaking to each of them to find out if they have an alibi and then asking them if they have a theory as to who the killer might be. I'm assuming the police will be doing the same thing. Who knows; maybe they'll figure it out before we do and we can get back to our family vacation."

"That would be nice. While I very much want to know who killed Mrs. Potter I find I don't have the enthusiasm for the hunt I usually do."

Zak got up from the computer and sat next to me on the bed. "We could just let the police handle this one. There are only a handful of suspects. I'm sure they'll figure it out."

I took a deep breath and let it out slowly. "No. I found the body and right now I'm the main suspect. I feel like I'm supposed to be involved. I know we have chaperone duties tomorrow, but most of our assignments involve helping out a member of the paid staff, so maybe we can just subtly question whoever we're working with."

Zak leaned in and kissed my cheek. "Okay." He placed a hand on my still-flat stomach. "But be careful. I wouldn't want anything to happen to either of my girls."

I smiled. "I'll be careful." I glanced at the computer. "Did you manage to get a signal?"

"I've got one. Where should we start?"

I paused to consider. "I suppose we should just see what we can find out about each of the suspects: what they do when they aren't at the camp; whether any of them have criminal records. We should find out if any of them knew Mrs. Potter outside the confines of the camp, and if they did, what their relationship was like."

Zak got up and went back to his computer. "Where do you want to start?"

"Let's start at the top, with Gina Keebler."

Zak was able to find out that Gina was thirty-six and was a counselor in a public school when camp wasn't in session. She'd worked at the camp for fourteen summers before this one and as a school guidance counselor for ten years. She'd never been married or had children and didn't have a criminal record. Zak wasn't able to find much information about how she spent her spare time, though it looked as if she liked to cook and had, in fact, co-authored a cookbook with a woman named Lorie Bell, who owned a restaurant in Chicago. Zak wasn't sure yet how the women knew each other because Gina had lived in Bryton Lake for all her adult life.

The only red flag this information provided was the cookbook. Mrs. Potter, whose first name, we learned, was Betty, had been the cook at the camp for twelve years and also had authored a cookbook, hers geared to meals for large groups. Could the two women have been engaged in some sort of argument over a recipe or the source or ownership of a recipe?

Zak next pulled up information on Seth Greenway. He was thirty-four and had worked at the camp for six previous summers. He was single and childless, though it looked like he'd been engaged some years back. Seth also lived in Bryton Lake and worked as a recreation worker for the local YMCA. On the surface, we didn't find any information that showed up as a red flag, but we both felt there might be something going on between him and Gina that could have led to a team effort to get Mrs. Potter out of the way should there have been an issue regarding a recipe, as I'd speculated.

Felix Manson was a tall, incredibly thin thirty-two-year-old with thin lips and small eyes. He seemed intelligent and Zak found he was a college graduate with a degree in finance. He worked at the camp during the summer and for a trucking company the rest of the year. The main thing that struck me about that was that neither career seemed the obvious choice for someone with his major. Zak wondered if there were legal problems in his past that prevented him from working in finance and was going to dig deeper into that possibility when we'd gathered basic profiles of our suspects. Of course, this was all simply speculation at this point that would need to be proven or disproven with additional research.

Darrell Ball was a twenty-six-year-old physical education teacher and baseball coach. He'd worked for his local high school for the past two years and the summer camp for the past five. Zak didn't find a criminal record and nothing jumped out as odd about his career choice, degree, or marital status; like the others, he was single with no children. We had no theory regarding why Darrell might have wanted Mrs. Potter dead should it turn out he was the killer.

Gordy Sinclair was a twenty-eight-year-old high school dropout who seemed to change jobs almost as often as he changed his socks. He was single with no children and moved around a lot. The only constant in his life was that he'd been a counselor at the camp for the past four years. I found it interesting that someone like Polly, whose last name was Vanhousen, would be messing around with someone like him, given that she currently attended an exclusive private college and was indeed engaged to the son of a very wealthy friend of her family. If I had to guess, Polly's employment at the camp as well as her apparent dalliance with Gordy was most likely her attempt at rebelling against her parents and spreading her wings a bit before settling down into married life with her upper-class counterpart. As for possible motives, I imagined a scenario in which Mrs. Potter knew Polly was messing around with Gordy and threatened to tell her parents or fiancé, which could have made Polly feel she had no choice but to remove the possible threat to her future.

Susan Kellogg was twenty-four years old and had worked at the camp for the past three years. She was currently working as an activities director for a high school. Our initial search into her personal life didn't reveal any motives for wanting Mrs. Potter out of it.

We didn't know the last name of Fred the janitor, though he was listed in the camp catalog, along with the counselors. Unfortunately, only his first name appeared below his photo, so an investigation into his life would have to wait for another day.

I got up from the bed, where I'd been sitting, and looked out the cabin's small window. "It looks like a beautiful night. Are you up for a walk to the lake?"

"I am if you are," Zak said, logging off his computer.

"I could use some fresh air before turning in. Let me just grab a sweatshirt."

Charlie trotted just ahead of us as Zak and I walked hand in hand, enjoying the reflection of the moon on the lake and the sound of crickets chirping in the forest all around us. We didn't talk much, just simply strolled along the narrow stretch of dirt lining the lake, enjoying each other's company while left alone with our private thoughts. We'd been walking for about twenty minutes when we paused to look out over the glossy surface of the lake.

"What do you think that is?" I pointed to something floating on the water several yards off the shore.

"I'm not sure." Zak looked around for a minute, then finally settled on a long, narrow tree branch, which he used to fish the object from the water.

"What is it?" I asked.

"An apron. Based on the size and the blood on the front, I assume it belonged to Mrs. Potter."

I thought back to the scene that afternoon. Mrs. Potter hadn't been wearing an apron. "Why would someone stab her and take her apron but leave her body and the murder weapon behind?"

Zak glanced at me with a frown. "I have no idea, but I have to wonder if anything else was dumped in the lake as well."

Chapter 3

Thursday, May 25

I woke the following morning with a slight feeling of queasiness but nothing like I'd been experiencing so far in my pregnancy. Maybe Ellie was correct when she'd tried to tell me that my symptoms had more to do with the stress of keeping such a huge secret from Zak rather than the baby growing in my womb. Zak had gotten up early and headed over to the cafeteria to help the counselors serve breakfast, which, like the previous evening's dinner, had been delivered from town in brown takeout boxes. I wasn't sure how long the kitchen would be taped off, but I wondered whether there would be someone to cook the food even when it was available for use.

I dressed in denim shorts and a bright yellow tank top and headed outdoors with Charlie to enjoy the beauty of the morning. Although I was feeling a bit better, I wasn't up for a big or greasy meal, so I grabbed a handful of crackers to take on my stroll in favor of eating in the cafeteria.

I'd thought a lot about the apron we'd found in the lake the previous evening. Zak had called Officer Michaelson, the police officer who'd interviewed him the day before, and told him about the apron, which led to the police closing the lake to activates for the day so they could dredge it to see if there was anything else to find.

As I watched the police launch a boat into the lake, one thing stood out in my mind: why? Why would anyone stab a woman and then take her apron only to leave it in the lake? It made no sense whatsoever. I couldn't see how the apron would provide any evidence beyond that which was provided already by the body and the murder weapon, so why go to all the trouble of removing and disposing of it?

"Unless…" I said aloud. Suddenly a lightbulb went off. The only reason I could think of to remove the apron but leave the body was if the DNA of the killer somehow had found its way onto it. Maybe Mrs. Potter had scratched her assailant. Maybe not all the blood on the apron belonged to her.

I wanted to share my theory with Zak, so I headed to the cafeteria. The room was packed to capacity with energized kids talking and laughing at the top of their lungs. Talk about loud! I guess I should have expected that a hundred-plus eleven- and twelve-years-olds would create a racket, but even in my wildest imagination I hadn't expected the degree to which my eardrums begged for mercy. I winced and put my hands over my ears to ward off the headache I could already feel developing. I paused near the entrance and looked around, hoping to spot Zak in the crowd. I finally found him sitting at a table with Scooter and maybe twenty other sixth-grade boys. I waved to get his attention without having to venture farther into the room with Charlie, but he was occupied with the kids and didn't see me. It was Alex, sitting with a group of girls not far from him, who eventually saw me and went over to Zak's table. I watched as she tapped on his shoulder, then pointed in my direction. Zak followed Alex's finger with his eyes and waved at me. He said something to Scooter before standing up and walking in my direction.

Taking my hand, he led me out into the sunshine. "You're up. I figured you'd sleep longer. How do you feel?"

"Not great, but not bad. Better than I have been."

"That's good, I guess. Do you want something to eat? They brought in breakfast sandwiches from town."

I put a hand on my stomach. "No, I'm good. I came to find you because I've thought some more about the apron and it occurred to me that the killer might have taken off the apron because it had somehow gotten their DNA on it."

Zak stopped walking to look at me. "You think Mrs. Potter fought back? Maybe she scratched or in some way injured her attacker and in the process got the killer's blood on her apron?"

I shrugged. "It's a theory."

"And a good one. We know she realized she was in trouble because she called 911 before she was stabbed. Or at least we assume it was before she was stabbed. And if she knew she was in trouble she would most likely have prepared herself to fight off her attacker. It seems she hid in the storage room, which her attacker was able to get in to. She might have given the 911 operator some indication of what was going on. I wonder if we can find out what she said during the call."

"Do you think the detective will tell us?"

"Probably not," Zak replied. "We don't have a relationship with the local PD like we do with Salinger back home. Still, I might be able to find out. Additionally, we know Mrs. Potter's body fell in a way that blocked the door and we suspect the killer went out the window. If that's true and the killer was injured in some way maybe we'll find blood on or near that window."

"I don't remember seeing any blood, but I didn't look all that closely either. I'm sure the police must have checked, but I still think we should take a second look. Maybe they missed something."

Zak glanced at the yellow tape. "No. I don't want either of us to end up in jail. I'll call Officer Michaelson again to tell him our theory. Maybe I can get him to share any evidence they've found."

Taking a passive role in this investigation wasn't sitting well with me, but Zak was right; getting tossed in jail for the weekend wasn't something I wanted to deal with.

Zak made his call and we headed to the camp office, where the assignments for the day had been posted. I saw immediately that while Zak had been given several groups to oversee throughout the day, I hadn't been assigned anything.

"Do you think Gina is afraid I really did kill Mrs. Potter?" I asked Zak.

He took out his phone and entered his schedule for the day. "Probably not. Chances are she wasn't sure how you'd be feeling after everything that happened yesterday, and I might have let it slip that you're pregnant as well."

I raised an eyebrow.

"I don't want you to overdo," Zak defended himself.

"I'm pregnant, not sick. I can pull my own weight. Still, not having any assignments today might work out well for me. It'll give me time to make the rounds and talk to people."

A look of concern crossed Zak's face. "You'll be careful?"

"I will." I looked at the assignment chart and considered my options. "I think I'll start with Polly. She's a tiny little thing. I'm sure I could take her if I had to."

Zak frowned. "You need to avoid any type of physical altercation. I know you're tough, but you could hurt the baby."

"I was kidding. Geez, lighten up."

Zak looked hurt by my comment. Maybe I was being harsh. It was natural that he'd be worried about me given my condition. I placed my hand on his arm. "I'm sorry. I guess I'm a little cranky this morning. I'll be careful, I promise. Polly's working with a group who'll be making picture frames out of items they gather in the forest. All I'm going to do is talk to her. Get to know her a bit. I don't plan to confront her or accuse her of anything. She'll be with kids, after all. Okay?"

He didn't answer at first.

"Come on, Zak. I'm just going to make a picture frame. It seems pretty safe."

Zak tucked a lock of hair that had fallen from my ponytail behind my ear before kissing the tip of my nose. "Okay. But keep your phone with you and give me a call after you speak to her. If you suspect anything at all don't confront her."

"I won't get myself into a dangerous situation. I swear. Why don't you take Charlie fishing with your group? I'm sure he'd enjoy hanging out with the kids and getting some exercise."

Zak leaned in and kissed me on the lips this time. "Okay. And remember, be careful."

I really hoped Zak wasn't going to be so überprotective for my entire pregnancy. If so, it was going to be a long eight months.

******

Polly Vanhousen was a petite blonde with bright blue eyes, a pert nose, wide lips, and a perfect complexion that bespoke regular facials and her upper-class upbringing. She smiled frequently and appeared to be friendly and approachable, and the girls in her group seemed to adore her. After a brief comment regarding my overwhelming desire to make a pinecone-rimmed photo frame for my best friend back home, I settled in with my supplies and got right to work.

I eased into conversation by talking to the girls about their projects and who they intended to give them to. I'd already shared my plans for my own frame while Polly had gotten everyone started. When all the girls were busy she settled onto the bench next to me, giving me the opening I needed.

"What a lovely ring. If it were mine I'd be afraid to lose it or, in the case of this particular project, get glue all over it." I held up my own bare left hand. "I left my rings behind for just that reason."

Polly shrugged. "It's just a ring. If I lose this one I'm sure Damian would buy me another."

"I think someone mentioned you're engaged to Damian Worthington the Third."

"Yes. That would seem to be the case."

Seem to be the case? That was an odd way of putting it. "Is there a problem? You sound bored by the idea."

Polly grinned, which didn't fit at all with her next words. "Oh, I am. Bored, bored, bored. But there isn't a thing to be done about it."

"What do you mean? Surely you don't have to marry him if you don't want to. People get engaged and then change their mind all the time."

Polly passed the girl sitting across from her a tube of glitter. "You don't get it. I can't change my mind. In fact, the choice wasn't really mine to begin with. Damian, who's the son of my father's best friend, was unofficially betrothed to me when I was just a baby."

I frowned. "You're having an arranged marriage?"

"Not arranged exactly. It's more like Damian and I have been thrown together since we were toddlers. Our parents have been drilling into our heads that we'd eventually wed. We know our parents can't legally force us to marry, and it certainly isn't required by our religion or culture, but if I broke things off with Damian my dad would not only be crushed, he'd probably cut me off financially."

"You'd marry your fiancé for money?"

Polly lifted a shoulder. "Sure. Why not? I like him; we get along well. And I adore the lifestyle my father's money provides. Damian and I have discussed the situation and we realize it's best for both of us not to rock the boat when there isn't any reason not to get hitched. It's not like I'm in love with anyone else, and neither is he."

"I see," I said, although I really didn't.

"I'll miss helping out at the camp. I applied for the counselor position last year as my one and only act of rebellion, but I found I really enjoyed working with the kids. My parents weren't thrilled that I decided to come back to the camp again this summer, but I pointed out to them that once I graduate college and get hitched to Damian, filling my days with things I enjoy will no longer be an option."

I sat back in my chair and considered the woman next to me. "If you feel that way why not wait to see if you find something you're passionate about—or even some*one* you're passionate about—rather than marrying someone who's been chosen for you?"

Polly looked at me. "You're married to Zak Zimmerman."

"Yes. That's right.

"He's even richer than my father. I'm sure he provides you with a lifestyle most women only dream of."

"Yes, but I fell in love with Zak because of him, not because of his money. I would have married him even if he'd been poor."

"Have you ever been poor?"

"No. Not really."

"Me neither, and being poor isn't an experience I'd choose to experience. There are things I'll have to give up to maintain my lifestyle, like working with the kids and a chance at real love, but in the end giving them up is much preferable to the alternative." Polly glanced at my picture frame, which I'd been working on as we talked. "You should put some shellac over the top once the glue dries. It'll help to preserve it, plus it'll make it look shiny."

I nodded, and Polly turned to speak to the girl sitting on her other side, effectively ending our conversation. I hadn't had the chance to ask her about Gordy, although asking her in front of the girls wouldn't have been a good idea anyway. Still, based on what Polly had shared, I now knew she valued her relationship with Damian at least for the lifestyle it would provide. If she was messing around with Gordy, as I suspected, and Mrs. Potter had found out about it and either threatened to tell her father or her fiancé or demanded some sort of payout for being quiet, I could see how sweet little Polly could have morphed into a cold-blooded killer.

As soon as I finished my picture frame, which had turned out awesome, I left the group and went in search of Zak, who, if I remembered correctly, had taken his group fishing in the river because the police had closed the lake for dredging. I wasn't sure in which direction they'd headed and Zak wasn't answering his cell, so I decided to walk upstream for a bit. If they weren't there I'd just catch up with him later in the day.

As I walked through the camp toward the river, I passed groups of kids playing volleyball, pitching horseshoes, building bird houses, and gathering flowers. The main attraction for the campers was always the swimming, canoeing, and paddle boarding the lake provided, so I hoped for their sake the police would complete their dredging operation before the next day, so those activities wouldn't have to be canceled.

It was early in the year, so the river was full and rushing rapidly. I could hear the falls in the distance and realized it was unlikely Zak would have headed in this direction unless he'd gone on past the rushing water. I thought about turning back but was enjoying my stroll with the warm sensation of the sun on my back and a slight cooling breeze in my face. I'd just arrived at the last bend before the falls when I heard voices. At first, I assumed it was Zak's group and hurried forward, but then I realized it wasn't Zak I heard but a pair of adults whose voices I didn't recognize immediately. I slipped behind a large tree trunk I figured would hide my small frame unless someone came down the trail. I quieted my mind and focused my attention on the conversation.

"I think she may turn out to be a problem," a female voice I was soon sure was Gina's stated.

"I think you're reading more into this than is warranted," a male voice answered. "Has she actually said anything to you?"

I wasn't 100 percent sure, but I figured the man was either Seth or possibly Fred the janitor. I hadn't heard Fred speak yet, but the voice certainly didn't belong to proper and curt Felix and I'd seen both Gordy and Darrell with their groups near the cabins when I walked by. The new counselors who'd shown up with the campers the previous afternoon were female, so it had to be Seth or Fred.

"No, but I think we might want to take precautions just in case." The longer I listened, the more certain I was that the female voice was Gina's.

"I hear what you're saying, darlin', but timing is key, so maybe we should wait to be sure our ducks are in a row."

Ducks in a row? What ducks? I didn't hear the woman's reply, but she must have disagreed because the next thing I knew someone came stomping down the trail, making me dive behind a large shrub to avoid detection. I waited, perfectly still, for the second person to follow. After a few minutes, I realized he must have gone off in the opposite direction because he never showed up.

I used my hands to slowly leverage my body into a sitting position. Not only had I gotten dark mud all over my butt but I'd scraped my palms and scratched my legs below my shorts as well. I flinched as I tried to stand, realizing I'd twisted my ankle when I dove to avoid detection. I didn't think it was sprained, but I'd need to baby it a bit on my trek back to the cabin, which would make it longer.

I swatted at a mosquito on my neck as I tried to wipe the mud from my shorts. I was sure that from a distance it was going to look like there was more going on back there than a slip and fall. I groaned as I took the first step on my sore ankle. There was no doubt about it; sleuthing in the forest was something best left to the bears.

******

An hour later I sat on a lawn chair in front of the cabin Zak and I shared. I'd managed to sneak back with only a few snickers from young campers whispering about the dark spot on the back of my shorts. Once I'd washed up and changed, I raided my chocolate stash to make up for the breakfast I'd never eaten and the lunch I most likely was going to skip. Armed with sweet, chocolaty goodness, I'd found a place in the shade for my chair and settled in to call Jeremy for an update about the goings-on at the Zoo.

"I hear congratulations are in order," he jumped right in after answering.

"I see the rumor mill is operating at full capacity. How'd you find out so soon?"

"I already suspected, as had Levi. We'd actually discussed the situation on a number of occasions. Ellie finally confirmed Levi's suspicions last night and he called me this morning to fill me in. Seriously, though, I'm very happy for you and Zak. You're such wonderful parents."

I smiled. "Thanks. I'm very happy, and Zak is too."

"Don't worry about a thing at the Zoo. You know I'll take care of everything while you're out on maternity leave."

"That won't be for a while, but honestly, you're pretty much running things now and I know you'll continue to do so. And you know how much I appreciate everything you do for me and the Zoo. I don't know what I'd do without you."

"Aw, shucks. Thanks. You know how much I love my job."

"I do. And I know I don't have to worry when I'm away. The reason I called today, though, was to get an update on the new bear cubs. Did they arrive?"

"They did and both seem to be settling in just fine. I got a call from the forest service about housing a cougar that was found on the side of the road after being hit by a car. We've been using the large cat enclosure for the bear cub overflow, but we'd talked about adding onto the bear enclosure with another room when the weather cleared a bit. I have a buddy who's a contractor and can do it right away if I get the green light."

I tucked one bare foot up under my leg. "I'm all for expanding, but it sounds like the cougar needs a home now."

"She does, but she isn't ambulatory yet and won't be for at least a few weeks. I spoke to Scott and he's willing to keep her at his facility for a bit while she's sedated anyway." Scott Walden was the veterinarian for both Zoe's Zoo and the town of Ashton Falls. "I figure that will give us time to add onto the bear enclosure and move the cubs before she begins to get around and requires the larger space."

"Okay," I decided. "If you can work out the details go for it. Anything else going on?"

"We've got coyotes in the campground just outside the town limits again. There are only a few campers this early, but the coyotes seem to be willing to brave human contact to scavenge the food they're leaving behind. I went over there this morning and spoke to everyone I could find about the proper handling of food and trash. Hopefully we won't have the same problems we had last year."

"Keep an eye on it," I instructed. "We don't want anyone else getting bit. It might not hurt to have Tank and Gunnar do a sweep through the area just after sunset." Tank and Gunnar Rivers were two brothers who worked the graveyard shift at the Zoo so there was supervision there twenty-four hours a day.

"Did we ever catch up with the stray the merchants on Main have been complaining about?" I asked, referring to the golden retriever we'd been trying to find for several weeks.

"Not yet. I've been making a sweep a couple of times a day, but she's a skittish one. I got a good look at her last night and I'm pretty sure she's pregnant. I'm going to talk to the merchants about calling me the next time she shows up rather than shooing her away."

"Poor thing." I always felt bad for animals who hadn't managed to find a forever home. "Let me know if you have any problems with the merchants. I'll speak to them personally if I have to. Maybe we can even get someone to lure her inside with food so it'll be easier to snare her. Ask Gilda Reynolds. She has a soft spot for all creatures great and small."

"Good idea. I'll pop into Bears and Beavers tomorrow while I'm out doing my regular sweep along Main Street."

I spoke to Jeremy for a few more minutes and then signed off. It seemed mini doughnuts I'd been nibbling had magically disappeared while I was on the phone. Crumpling up the now-empty bag, I headed into the cabin to search for the half-bag of Oreos I knew were left from the previous evening. I usually ate fairly healthily, but it seemed baby Catherine was a chocoholic if there ever was one.

Chapter 4

Zak and Charlie came back to the cabin shortly after I polished off the remaining cookies. Charlie was thrilled to see me but obviously exhausted from the hike, so once he greeted me he jumped up onto the bed, found a comfy spot at the bottom, and went to sleep.

"What happened to your leg?" Zak asked when he noticed the scratches.

"I had a run-in with a thorny bush, but I'm fine. How was fishing?"

"Not as good as it would have been in the lake, but not bad. Darrell is helping the kids who caught fish clean them. We'll grill them tonight along with the hamburgers Gina is planning to BBQ because the kitchen is still closed." He grabbed a bottle of water from our stash.

"It looks like someone had chocolate for breakfast."

I shrugged. "What can I say? Catherine is a chocoholic. Do you have another group this afternoon?"

"Not until three. Would you like to drive into town for lunch? I think the kids are having bologna and cheese sandwiches."

A salad with fresh greens and a light dressing sounded a lot better than bologna and cheese. "That would be nice." I glanced at Charlie. "Do you think he'll be okay?"

"I think he'll be out cold for at least a few hours. Trying to keep up with ten twelve-year-old boys about did him in."

I called Alex to tell her what we were doing. I felt a little bad not inviting her to come, but she assured me that she was having the time of her life. She also offered to check in on Charlie in an hour or so. If he was awake she would take him with her on the nature walk she and some of the girls were taking that afternoon. I thanked her for her offer and told her to text me if that ended up being what she did so I'd know for certain.

Zak found a cute café with an outdoor patio right on the river. I ordered a green salad with a baked chicken breast and Zak chose a prime rib sandwich. It was a beautiful day, with temperatures in the midseventies, perfect for outdoor dining.

As we waited for our food, I filled Zak in on my conversation with Polly.

"That's really sad," he said about her decision to marry for money and security rather than love. "If her fiancé knows the score they're at least in it together, but I used to be cautious about dating women who only cared about money before you and I got together."

"How did you know I wasn't one of them?"

Zak laughed. "Because you hated me on sight, and that was before I ever had any money. After all the work I had to do to get you to go out with me even one time, there was no doubt in my mind that my wealth hadn't swayed you in the least."

"I didn't hate you," I defended myself.

Zak raised an eyebrow.

"Okay, maybe I detested you a little bit, but I never hated you. In fact, I think I probably loved you all along despite how inconvenient that was for me at the time."

Zak placed his hand over mine. "I'm just glad the hero won in the end."

I grinned. "Yeah. Me too."

We paused when the server brought our food. She filled our water glasses and moved on, and I asked Zak if he'd had an opportunity to speak to any of the counselors that morning. He reported that Seth had gone with his group and he'd managed to work a few general questions into their conversation. I realized if Seth was with Zak it must have been Fred I'd overheard talking to Gina.

"What did you find out?" I asked, spearing a piece of fresh, crisp lettuce.

"That Seth and Gina are friends outside the confines of the camp. He swore that was as far as it ever went, but I'm not sure I completely believed him. He said she just took over the administrator job three years ago, when the previous one retired. And he also said Mrs. Potter's death wasn't the first one at the camp since he's been working there."

"Who else died?"

Zak finished chewing the bite he'd taken and set down his sandwich before he continued. "According to Seth, of the six summers he's already worked here, three other people have died."

I placed my hand on my heart. "I hope not any kids,"

Zak shook his head. "No. All three were adults. The first year Seth worked here one of the counselors—a twenty-two-year-old named Sarah—drowned while taking a late-night swim. The death was ruled an accident because the police didn't find any evidence of foul play and no one was seen accompanying her when she left the campfire early to return to her cabin."

"So she was at the campfire with everyone else and then decided to head back to her cabin early but ended up dead in the lake?"

"Apparently. Seth said her body wasn't found until the next day and it was never determined exactly when she died. Her cabinmates all reported that when they got there she'd already left, but they didn't know where she'd gone. There was speculation that she'd really left the campfire to hook up with one of the other counselors, but the police investigation revealed that the counselor everyone initially thought she'd gone off with was with two other people the entire evening, so it couldn't have been him."

"They could have lied to cover for him," I pointed out.

Zak nodded. "They could have. But there was no proof they did."

"Are any of the three friends still working here?"

"No," Zak confirmed. "According to Seth, none of them came back the following year."

It was possible Sarah simply had decided to go for a swim and drowned, but considering what had happened to Mrs. Potter and two other people, my Zodar was on full alert and I doubted that was the case. "You said there were other deaths in the past six years."

"The second person to die was another female counselor. Her name was Cleo and she was found dead in the woods after her cabinmates reported her missing earlier in the day. Cleo was a new counselor that year and it was only a week before the camp was going to close for the season. Seth told me the staff was tired and tension was running high. He said Cleo went to bed the previous evening at the usual time and slept in the bed she'd been assigned to. When the counselors in her cabin awoke in the morning they found her gone. Of course, at first everyone assumed she was using the bathroom or showering, but when she didn't show up for breakfast they started to look for her. When she hadn't been found by noon, even though she had classes to teach and field trips to chaperone, they organized a formal search party. Her body was found later that afternoon in a densely wooded area about a half mile from the main part of the camp."

I felt my stomach churn with dread. "How did she die?"

"It appeared she'd tripped over a tree branch and hit her head. Most likely that led to her blacking out and eventually bleeding to death."

I put my hand over my mouth.

"Too graphic?" Zak asked.

I nodded.

"Sorry. I forgot about your delicate stomach."

I took a deep breath through my nose and blew it out of my mouth. "No. That's okay. Being so squeamish isn't really setting well with me. We're investigating a murder. Things are going to get graphic." I took a sip of my water. "Did they ever figure out what she was doing in the woods in the first place?"

"No. It was determined she'd died between one and three a.m. No one knew why she would have been in the woods in the middle of the night."

"Did the police consider foul play?"

"Initially, but there was no evidence that would support it."

"I really don't like the sound of that," I commented. "I know these were both ruled accidents, but they seem suspicious."

"Yeah. It seems a pattern is beginning to emerge. When Seth told me about the third death before Mrs. Potter's, I was even more certain there could be something linking all of them. The thing is, the only staff members to have been around for them all are Gina and Seth, and I don't have any reason yet to suspect either of being a serial killer."

I thought of the conversation I'd overheard that morning between a woman I was fairly sure was Gina and a man I now suspected was Fred.

"What about the janitor? How long has Fred been around?"

Zak paused. "I didn't think to ask that. We should find out."

I planned to fill Zak in on the conversation I'd overheard, but first I wanted to find out about the third victim, so I asked him to continue.

"She was another woman and also a staff member, hired to oversee the arts and crafts program. She was a twenty-six-year-old artist named Wilma who'd agreed to work at the camp after returning to the States after a couple of years in Paris. Wilma had worked at the camp before going abroad but hadn't for the two summers before she died."

"Do I dare ask how she died?" I grimaced.

"She fell off a horse and broke her neck. According to the campers who were with her, the horse was spooked and took off at a run. Wilma wasn't an experienced rider and fell to her death after a valiant attempt to slow the horse."

"So it was also an accident."

"On the surface, it would seem so."

I took another deep breath and let everything sink in. Three women had died two, four, and six years ago. All three deaths appeared to have been accidents. Based on what we knew, the only staff working for the camp at the time of all three deaths were Gina and Seth. Gina had been instructing someone to "take care" of someone, which led me to believe she could very well be a killer. I hated to tell Zak the real reason my legs were scratched, but I realized that under the circumstances coming clean with him was the only option.

"I overhead a conversation a woman and a man were having while I was taking a walk this morning."

"A woman and a man? You don't know who?"

"I hid so as not to be detected. I never did see who they were, but I heard what they said. Or at least part of it. I'm fairly sure the woman was Gina, and while I can't be about the man, based on the process of elimination I think it may have been Fred."

"And what did they say?"

I filled Zak in.

"That could mean a lot of different things," he said, "but given the situation I don't like it. Did you have a sense of who they felt needed to be take care of or why?"

"No. I came into the conversation toward the end, I'm afraid."

Zak looked off into the distance, appearing to be mulling things over. I could see the emotions playing across his face as he took some time to process everything. Eventually, he looked at me and said, "The fact that these deaths all occurred two years apart originally led me to believe there was some sort of ritual killing going on, but now I'm not so sure. The conversation you overheard makes it sound as if Gina and whoever she was speaking to plan to carry out some action against some person for a very specific reason. And Mrs. Potter was obviously murdered; there was no attempt to make it appear to be an accident, which actually breaks the pattern of the other deaths."

"What if the killer had other plans but was interrupted? Mrs. Potter knew she was in trouble and made the 911 call herself. What if the killer had to make a quick change when it became clear the cops were on the way?"

"That's possible. But the fact that that conversation took place after Mrs. Potter's death makes it seem there's a second death looming and that would break the pattern as well."

I didn't respond. I didn't know what to say.

"Maybe we should take the kids and go," Zak said.

"What about the killer?"

"It isn't your job to find the killer. I know it's your natural inclination to do so, but we have three children including Catherine to think about."

Zak had a point, but the detective had warned me against leaving and I reminded Zak of that. "Besides, the kids should be safe. None of the victims were children. In fact, all of them were female staff members. There wasn't even a parent chaperone in the bunch."

"That's true, and on the surface, I can see how you might come to the conclusion that we're safe, but if there's going to be a second victim you can't count on that."

I couldn't disagree with him. "Okay; how about this?" I began. "Why don't we go to the police station to see if we can speak to either of the men who interviewed us? We can tell them what we've learned, see what they have to say, and then make a decision about what to do next."

Zak took a moment, then agreed. I figured as long as the police themselves weren't in on whatever was going on they might be willing to share their thoughts.

******

The detective who'd interviewed me wasn't available, but Officer Michaelson was at the station and was willing to speak to us. He seemed to be a nice enough guy and offered us a friendly smile, cold drinks, and the willingness to hear us out.

Zak explained what Seth had told him and our concern that Mrs. Potter's death could in some way be related to the deaths of the other three women. He took his time, offering all the information we had. In my opinion, he made a compelling case, but I could see by the look on Officer Michaelson's face that he wasn't buying any of it.

"I know Mrs. Potter's death has led to a lot of speculation, but I don't think it's connected to any of the other deaths at the camp. They were accidents."

"Maybe, but doesn't the fact that there were three accidents two years apart seem suspect to you?" I argued.

"I've lived in Duck Lake my whole life. I went to the camp when I was a kid and when I got older I was a counselor for two years before I was hired by the police department. A lot of weird stuff happens at the camp that no one other than the staff ever finds out about. While tragic, I assure you the deaths of those three women really were accidents, but if you still have concerns and would like to speak to Detective Swanson, you're welcome to leave a message for him and he'll get back to you when he can."

We didn't have much choice but to leave a message and hope the detective really would get back to us. As we left the police station, I called Sheriff Salinger to see if he had any way to get hold of the police reports for the three deaths Seth had told Zak about. He took down the names and dates and said he'd try but couldn't promise anything.

"What now?" Zak asked after I hung up with Salinger, who'd assured me he'd made a compelling case to Detective Swanson that I wasn't in any way involved in Mrs. Potter's death.

"I heard someone mention there's a small, semimonthly newspaper in town. It might be worth our while to talk to whoever owns it to see if they have anything to say about the three deaths."

"Sounds like a good idea," Zak said. "Do you know where the office is?"

"No. Why don't you Google it while I call Alex? I want to make sure everything's okay."

Zak located the newspaper office and started driving there while I chatted with Alex, who assured me that she and Scooter were having a wonderful time and Charlie was with them and seemed happy as well. I made her promise to call me if anything odd seemed to be going on and let her go.

Chapter 5

The *Duck Lake News* offered local advertising and covered local events. I wasn't certain how long it had been in operation, but based on the look of the outdated equipment in the office, it could have been quite a while. The current publisher introduced himself to us as Burt Parkenson. He was a tall man with short brown hair who looked to be in his early-to midthirties. We filled him in on the information we were after, and he told us he'd taken over the newspaper from his grandfather when he retired and had only been in charge himself for the past eighteen months. He was happy to help us dig up anything we needed on the earlier three deaths in exchange for an interview on the murder of Mrs. Potter for the article he was planning to write.

Unfortunately, the newspaper hadn't gone digital until after Burt took over, so the information we sought would need to be found via the old newspapers in the morgue, filed by date. At least it appeared as if there was a logical filing system, so it seemed locating specific editions wouldn't be all that difficult. Once the correct newspapers were located, Burt set Zak and me up at one of the long tables he used to stack bundles for the local racks.

In each of the three cases, Burt's grandfather had done a good job of piecing together what had occurred based on interviews with those involved combined with technical information from the police reports.

The articles basically confirmed what Seth had already told Zak. Sarah Collins had drowned six years ago, Cleo Thornton had fallen and hit her head while wandering in the woods in the middle of the night two years later, and Wilma Partridge had broken her neck after falling from a horse two years after that. All three deaths appeared to have been accidents; there was no evidence that foul play had been involved in any instance.

"Look at this," Zak said, pointing to one of the articles. "One of the campers who was with Wilma when she died said it appeared the horse was hit in the hindquarters by a flying object before it took off."

"A flying object? Like what?"

"According to the article, the ten-year-old didn't know. The other members of the riding group claimed they didn't see or hear anything, so her comment doesn't seem to have been given a lot of attention." Zak looked up at me.

"If something hit the horse hard enough to spook it, I'd think it would have left a welt or at least a mark of some sort. At the very least the investigator should have checked the horse for injuries. Maybe there's a notation in the police report. I hope Salinger will be able to get hold of the reports, which should give us a lot of additional information regarding the three deaths."

Zak and I continued to read. The only death to have occurred in the presence of witnesses was Wilma's fall from the horse. The other counselors appeared to have died late at night when they were alone. While I understood the fact that the police hadn't been able to come up with any evidence that would point to foul play, the circumstances behind the deaths seemed fishy to me.

Burt returned to the morgue, where we were still working a short time after he left us. "You folks find what you were looking for?"

"We found the articles, but they didn't provide much more information than we already had. By all accounts the three deaths were random accidents. Would everything the people who were interviewed have said been used in the articles?" I wondered.

"Probably not. Most times when researching an article you talk to a lot of folks but just use the material that fits the story you're writing."

"Would you keep your notes from the interviews?" I asked.

"I'm not a hundred percent certain, but I might have what you're after. Grandpa used to keep everything. If he had his handwritten notes they'd most likely be boxed up in the storage room out back. I can let you in if you want to look around, but be warned: It's dusty in there and I can't guarantee what you'll find."

I glanced at Zak, who shrugged. I turned back to Burt. "If you don't mind it wouldn't hurt to take a look."

"Follow me. The storage room is more of a garage, but the only things in it are boxes and boxes of notes and correspondence."

The room was detached from the main building where the newspaper was published, but I saw what Burt meant when he'd said it was more of a garage. There was a large door leading out to the alley, which I imagined had allowed access to an automobile at one time. He let us in through a small door in the side, flicking a switch by the door to turn on the light.

"The boxes are labeled with date ranges, but I can't guarantee they're stacked in order. It seems Grandpa started at the back and then stacked more recent boxes to the front. I'll be working on an article in my office, but give me a holler if you need anything."

"Thanks; we will." I smiled.

"And don't forget to come back through the main building so we can chat about the recent death for my article."

"We won't forget," I promised.

I stood near the door and looked around the room, which was piled with boxes in every direction. "Where do we start?"

"The boxes are marked and it appears the dates are easy to find. I guess we should just start walking around and when one of us sees a date range that corresponds to one of the deaths at the camp we'll holler."

"We're looking for dates between the end of May and the end of August two, four, and six years ago. Hopefully the boxes we need will be near the front."

The first promising box we located was from four years back, when Cleo Thornton was found dead in the woods. A lot of the staff members who were interviewed then no longer worked for the camp, so I didn't have a sense of who these people were, but I knew Gina, Seth, Gordy, Felix, and Darrell had worked there then and could quite possibly have spoken to Burt's grandfather.

"It looks like the information given by Gina was fairly detailed," Zak said after reading one of the handwritten notes. "Just as Seth said, Cleo went to bed as she did every night, but when the girls in her cabin woke up the next morning she was missing. When she didn't show up by noon a thorough search of the property was initiated and Cleo's body was eventually found in a heavily wooded area. Mr. Parkenson asked Gina if Cleo had been involved in a romantic relationship with anyone she may have snuck off to meet, and she said she may have had a thing going on with one of the newer counselors, Gordy Sinclair."

I raised an eyebrow. "Gordy gets around. He hooked up with Cleo during his first summer and now he seems to be messing around with Polly."

"We don't know for certain he's been messing around with anyone," Zak reminded me. "Still, if it does turn out he was meeting Cleo, he'd be a strong suspect if it turned out she was intentionally pushed onto the rock she hit her head on rather than simply tripping and falling, as the police eventually determined."

"If Gina mentioned Gordy to Burt's grandfather, chances are he interviewed him as well. See if you can find the notes associated with that interview," I instructed Zak.

It took him a minute to locate them.

"Gordy admitted he and Cleo were seeing each other and had arranged to meet at midnight down by the lake. When she hadn't shown up by twelve-thirty he assumed she wasn't able to get away and went back to his own cabin. He told Burt's grandfather he had no idea why Cleo had gone into the woods or where she'd been between one and three a.m., the time investigators estimated she died."

"If she died from a head wound she could very well have tripped and hit her head at midnight but not died right away," I pointed out. "Of course, that still wouldn't explain why she was in the woods if she'd snuck out to meet Gordy at the lake."

"Maybe she snuck out at midnight with plans to meet Gordy but then saw or heard something that caused her to veer into the woods," Zak suggested.

I sat back and narrowed my eyes. "It could have happened that way, but another possibility is that Gordy was lying. Don't you think he might have lured her into the woods and then killed her, making it look like an accident?"

"I don't know. We obviously just met him, but he seems like a nice enough guy. Though I guess even people with pleasant personalities can have a violent side."

Zak returned to sorting thought the box. He handed me several interviews with people who were no longer with the camp to read. Only one of them mentioned the Gordy and Cleo connection. I supposed the couple could have been careful to keep their romance to themselves.

"Here's an interview with Darrell Ball," Zak announced. "He says Cleo seemed serious and distracted for the whole week prior to her accident. Darrell's such a huge goofball, his description of serious behavior could just mean she wasn't running around doing cartwheels, but it might be worth looking in to. Maybe there was something going on that no one knew about."

"We could ask both Gordy and Darrell about Cleo. We still need to interview them about Mrs. Potter anyway. We can ask them about the woman who fell off the horse as well. They both were working at the camp two years ago. Did you notice whether Felix was interviewed? It would have been his first summer there four years ago."

Zak finished sorting through that box but didn't find interviews with either Felix or Seth. Polly and Susan wouldn't have been working at the camp yet, so he set that box aside and we began a search for the box containing notes about either Sarah Collins or Wilma Partridge. After a few minutes, I found the one that, based on the date range written on the exterior, should contain the notes regarding Wilma's fall from the horse.

Zak grabbed it, which was on top of five other boxes, and set it on the floor. He took off the lid and began to sort through.

"Here we go," he said, pulling out a manila envelope. "It looks like all the notes are in here." Zak handed me a stack of notes and I began to read. As with the previous death, there were notes from interviews with people whose names I didn't recognize. I did, however, find some from Gina's interview in which she revealed that Gordy had shown a romantic interest in Wilma.

Coincidence? I thought not. "Look at this," I said to Zak.

"This is too bizarre. There has to be a link between Gordy's interest in these women and their eventual deaths."

"Wilma wasn't at the camp the year before her death," I said. "In fact, if I remember correctly, she didn't work at the camp the two years prior to her death, although she'd worked there before her trip to Paris. I wonder if Gordy had a romantic interest the year when no death occurred."

"We'd have to ask him or someone else who was around then."

"I think an even better question is, if Gordy and Wilma actually did have a thing going on, as Gina indicated, and he has something going on with Polly now, is she in some sort of danger?"

"That could be a possibility. We need to figure this out fast. Have you found notes from an interview with Gordy?"

I sorted through. "No. Do you have them?"

Zak quickly looked through his pile. "No. You'd think someone would have realized there was a link between Gordy and the dead girls and asked him about it. Even if the detective who investigated Wilma's death was someone different from the one who investigated Cleo's, Gina or Burt's grandfather must have made the connection."

"Maybe the interview with Gordy is somewhere else or he refused to be interviewed. There should be something in the police file anyway, if we ever manage to get our hands on it. Did you find anything from the camper who thought she saw something hit the horse before it took off?"

"No. I haven't found notes in this envelope from interviews with any campers, only staff. Maybe there's another envelope or folder somewhere." Zak glanced at his watch. "I need to get back to camp for my three o'clock group and we promised we'd speak to Burt. Maybe he'll let us come back tomorrow to take another look if we haven't figured things out by then."

We put everything back where we'd found it and went into the office to find Burt. Zak let him know we didn't have long to answer questions so he should ask the most important ones up front, and if he had anything else he could either call us or we could come back after Zak finished his duties for the day. Fortunately, Burt was organized and knew exactly what he was after. Most of his questions were for me because I was the one who'd found Mrs. Potter in the pantry.

Once I'd told him what I could, Zak and I stopped at the minimart to restock my chocolate stash, then headed back to the camp. I wasn't sure whether Gordy had a group that afternoon or if he was off for a shift as Zak had just been, but I definitely wanted to speak to him before the end of the day, so I went over to the volunteer board to see who was off and who was on that afternoon.

It looked like Gordy had a group but would be done in a half hour and off after that until he was scheduled to take his campers to dinner at six. That would give me a couple of hours to track him down and, hopefully, interview him. I wanted to speak to Gina too, but it looked like she was tied up until after the evening campfire, while Darrell was currently camper free, and he'd been around when both Cleo and Wilma died. Where could I find him?

The lake was still closed, but the pool was open, so I started there. If I couldn't find him I'd ask around. Maybe someone had seen him.

"Nice day today," I said conversationally to Susan Kellogg, the only counselor I found at the pool. She was supervising a group of girls, so I sat down next to her.

"It really is a great day. I hoped it would be sunny but not too hot. Last year it went from winter to summer and skipped spring entirely."

"Seems like a perfect temperature for swimming. I hope they get the lake open by tomorrow." I kicked off my flip-flops and stretched out my legs so I could take advantage of the afternoon rays while I was chatting.

"I heard they plan to have it open. I'm pretty sure they didn't find anything else. If they did no one is saying so. The whole thing is just too weird. And disturbing. Who would kill Betty? It makes no sense."

"Do you know how long she'd been with the camp?" I asked.

"A long time. I think almost as long as Gina. She had her moments when she'd let her impatience get the better of her, but overall, she was a nice lady everyone seemed to get along with. I can't think of a single staff person who would do what someone obviously did. It makes me wonder if there's a vagrant in the area."

"A vagrant?"

"This is the first group at the camp this season and Mrs. Potter died on the first day she was here. It makes me wonder if someone wasn't squatting on the grounds over the winter. Maybe Mrs. Potter stumbled onto them and they killed her."

I hadn't considered that possibility, but now I realized Susan had a point. It was possible the killer was someone who'd been in the area but not associated with the camp. Until now I'd been focused on the eight staff members whose whereabouts I was uncertain of when Mrs. Potter was stabbed.

I decided to dive right in. "I understand Mrs. Potter wasn't the first person to die here."

"That's true. There was a woman two years ago. Although she wasn't murdered like Mrs. Potter. She fell off a horse and broke her neck."

"Still. It must have been tragic."

"It was upsetting," Susan agreed. "Thankfully, it happened at the very end of the summer, so camp let out and we all went home shortly after."

"Someone told me that someone might have thrown something at the horse that made him bolt."

"No, I don't think so. I wasn't with the group, but I'm pretty sure the horse took off for no reason whatsoever."

"So the horse wasn't well trained?"

Susan shook her head. "No, he was. He'd been with the camp for five years and there'd never been a problem with him before." I noticed the frown that crossed Susan's face. "You know, now that you mention it, it does make sense that the horse was prompted to bolt. The girls who'd been on the ride all said they hadn't seen anyone in the area, but Darrell had had a group of his boys make slingshots during craft time. I remember it because we argued when I said a slingshot wasn't a craft. He didn't agree…but I digress. The point is, that group of boys were making everyone nuts with those dang things. I suppose it wouldn't be out of the realm of possibility to suggest that the kids were playing nearby, shooting rocks at targets as they'd been doing all week, and one of the rocks could have taken a wild path and hit the horse." Susan looked at me. "I wonder if that was ever explored."

I shrugged. "I don't know, but it does make sense. It's even possible someone used a slingshot to hit the horse intentionally."

"Why would anyone do that?"

"Maybe to play a prank on Wilma. Did she have any enemies?"

Susan paused. "It was the end of the summer and there'd been a lot of squabbling going on. Everyone was tired by then, and the heat was unbearable. I don't know who all might have held a grudge against Wilma, but she and I hadn't been getting along all that well. The counselors are hired because we bring a talent to the camp, and mine happens to be overseeing the crafts the campers are assigned. Wilma was an artist who'd just come back from two years abroad and she was about as full of herself as a person could be. I'd spent the previous year establishing my niche with the camp and then she came along and wanted to take over. I was pretty angry with her by the end of the summer, but I would never have pulled such a mean, obviously dangerous prank. Everyone knew Wilma was skittish around the horses. In fact, I'm not even certain why she was on that ride. Gina tries not to assign anyone tasks they aren't competent in, so Wilma was never assigned a riding group."

"Maybe someone got sick at the last minute and she was asked to fill in?" I speculated.

"I guess that could have happened. Still, it seems as if they should have traded things around and worked it out so Wilma didn't have to ride."

"And Gina is always the one to assign the groups?"

"Sure, when she's here. If she isn't, and a change needs to be made, Seth would most likely do it." Susan looked back at the pool. "I need to get them out. It was nice talking to you."

"Thanks, you too."

Gordy would be free in just a few minutes, so I slipped on my flip-flops and headed in the direction where I thought I was most likely to run into him. A conversation with Darrell would have to wait for another time.

Chapter 6

I found Gordy sitting at a picnic table chatting with Polly when I arrived at the grassy area at the center of camp where I thought I'd be most likely to find him. I waved at the pair and walked in their direction.

"How's your first day going?" I asked as I approached them.

"So far so good," Polly answered. "Although I have a group in twenty minutes, so I should head over to the craft cabin to get set up." She glanced at Gordy. "See you later?"

He winked. "Count on it."

Polly headed off in the direction from which I'd just come and I turned to Gordy. "I know it's none of my business, but I get the impression you and Polly have a thing going on."

"We do," Gordy admitted without hesitation.

"You know she's engaged?"

He shrugged his shoulders.

"And it doesn't bother you that the woman you're involved with plans to marry another man?" I had to ask.

"Not in the least. My interest in Polly extends to the last day of camp. After that she can do whatever she wants."

I must have looked both shocked and confused because Gordy offered an additional explanation without my having to prompt him. "Look, I know there are people who might look at casual sex as a negative, but in my opinion, it's the best thing when spending the summer in an isolated situation. One of the first things I realized when I first accepted this job was that dating wasn't going to be possible for three months out of every year. Besides, I'm not interested in a serious relationship that would extend beyond the summer or carry forward any baggage."

"So you pick out women who are interested in a summer fling but nothing more?"

Gordy nodded. "Exactly. And I make it a policy not to have a sexual relationship with any woman for more than one summer."

"So every year you come to the camp and scout out your next conquest?" I asked with a tone of disgust.

"You make it sound bad, but it isn't. I treat my summer girls really well and never cheat. And I make sure they know the score up-front."

"Has there ever been a summer when there weren't any takers?"

"Not so far. I met Polly last summer, but she didn't start working here until I'd already come to an agreement with Evelyn. I knew Polly was interested, but like I said, I never cheat, so she and I came to an understanding that if she worked at the camp this year and was still interested, she'd have first dibs on all this." Gordy ran his hands from his head down to his knees on both sides of his body.

Ugh! What a sleazebag.

"So, I imagine after a year of anticipation, you and Polly connected right away?"

Gordy grinned. "Oh yeah. Polly and I were going at it from the minute Gina released us yesterday right up until the buses pulled in. I feel like I made a good choice. Even after three hours in heaven I find myself eager for more alone time with her."

If that were true it gave Polly and Gordy alibis for Mrs. Potter's death. I'd need to confirm things with Polly, but based on the look on Gordy's face I could see it was true. "And what happened to Evelyn?" I wondered.

"She decided not to work here this summer. We haven't kept in touch, but I think she must have gone abroad. She mentioned her plan several times last summer."

"Do the women you have your casual relationships with ever come back the next year?"

"Not so far."

Okay, I'd learned some disturbing things about Gordy, but I hadn't figured out a way to bring the dead women into the conversation yet. I needed to keep things casual and nonjudgy if I wanted him to open up to me.

I forced a smile and tried to relax my posture. "I guess I can understand what you're saying. It seemed sort of cold at first, but as long as the women you choose to have relationships with know the score I can see how getting involved with another staff person would make the summer more tolerable. Did you start this plan your very first year?"

Gordy nodded. "Yup, although I'll admit that first summer didn't work out as planned."

"And why was that?" I asked innocently.

"The girl I made plans with died."

"Died? What happened?"

"She tripped and hit her head. It was pretty bad. They found her body in the woods."

I offered a look of sympathy. "I'm so sorry. That must have been hard on everyone."

"It was." Gordy's expression momentarily communicated real grief that he quickly masked. "But things got better after that rocky start."

"So you've had a girl every year you've worked here?"

"I have. After Cleo there was Veronica, followed by Brenda, which led to Evelyn, and now Polly." Gordy leaned in just a bit. "I have an opening for next summer if you're interested."

Ew. "Thanks, but I'm married and intend to have it stay that way."

"Too bad. You'd remember a night with me forever."

Okay, now I was definitely going to puke.

"You look a little pale," Gordy said. "You okay?"

"Not really. My stomach has been kind of off. I think I'm going to go lay down, but before I do I wanted to ask you about Wilma. Someone mentioned to me that they'd remembered you'd hooked up with someone named Wilma."

Gordy smiled. "So you've been asking around about me. Maybe you aren't quite as immune to my charms as you'd like me to believe."

"No, it's not that. The person was telling me about the accident Wilma had and your name came up."

"If someone linked me with Wilma they were wrong. She wasn't the kind of girl to be interested in the type of relationship I'm offering. In fact, she was kind of a tight ass, if you know what I mean. I'm sorry about what happened to her, but she rubbed everyone the wrong way. When Cleo died everyone was really upset. When Wilma died, not so much."

The longer I spoke to Gordy the more nauseated I became, so I made my excuses and headed back to the cabin to lay down. When I arrived, Charlie was sleeping on the bed, so I pulled the curtains closed and cuddled up with him. It didn't take long before we were both fast asleep.

******

Zak arrived in the cabin several hours later to find Charlie and me snoring away. He must not have wanted to wake us because I caught him sneaking out with his sweatshirt over his arm.

"What time is it?" I asked.

"Eight," Zak answered as he came back inside, closing the door behind him.

"Eight? As in p.m.?"

"I'm afraid so. I wasn't sure whether I should wake you for dinner, but you were out cold, so I decided to let you rest. Charlie too. I was just heading out to the campfire. I'll wait for you if you want to go."

I rubbed my eyes with one hand and tried to wake up the rest of the way. If I didn't get up for a couple of hours I most likely wouldn't sleep through the night, which I wanted to do.

"I'd like to go to the campfire. Just give me a minute to change into something warmer and wash up. Are Alex and Scooter already there?"

"Yeah, they went over with their cabinmates."

Zak took Charlie out while I changed into jeans and a sweatshirt, then headed over to the communal bathrooms to wash up. By the time I returned to the cabin Zak had fed Charlie, who looked refreshed and energized after his long nap.

"You should eat something before we head over," Zak encouraged me. "You still have half your sandwich from last night."

I did feel hungry, so I nibbled the sandwich while I filled him in on my conversation with Gordy. "His attitude toward women didn't sit well with me, but he didn't appear to be hiding anything. I got the feeling he cared for Cleo and was saddened by her death, but when I brought up Wilma's name he made it very clear she wasn't the sort of woman he would be interested in hooking up with for his summer fling."

"Might he have killed her even if he wasn't sleeping with her?" Zak asked.

"Maybe, but what would be his motive? He didn't like her, but he suggested that most of the other counselors weren't huge fans either. I usually have a good sense when people are lying, and as far as I could tell he wasn't. I'm not sure I would take him off the suspect list at this point, but I'd move him down to the bottom. Susan too. Like Gordy, she admitted she didn't get along with Wilma, but she didn't appear to be holding anything back."

"Okay, so let's say neither Gordy nor Susan killed Wilma. Does it stand to reason they therefore didn't kill Mrs. Potter either?"

"No." I frowned. "I guess the two aren't necessarily connected. Initially, when you told me about the other three deaths I felt they had to be linked to Mrs. Potter's somehow, but now I'm not so sure. We don't even know if the other women were murdered. Maybe all three of them died as the result of unfortunate accidents." I glanced at Zak. "Maybe we should refocus a bit. It could be that Mrs. Potter's death was an isolated incident. If Gordy is telling the truth he was hooking up with Polly when Mrs. Potter was attacked, giving them alibis for her death at least. Maybe we should be working on getting everyone else's alibi too."

"Don't you think the police have already done that?"

"Yeah, they must have. We really need to get a look at the official report." I looked out the open window. "Salinger will already be off for the day so I won't be able to bug him until tomorrow. I don't suppose you'd want to skip the campfire and spend the evening hacking into the local law enforcement database?"

"Let's try talking to Salinger first," Zak suggested gently. "If there's a legal way to get the information we need I'd just as soon wait and do it that way."

I took a sip of water, then screwed the cap back on the top of the bottle. "You're right. It can wait. Let's go sing campfire songs and roast marshmallows. I'll put Charlie on his leash; it's almost dark and he isn't familiar with the area. I'd hate for him to get lost."

******

It was almost eleven by the time the gathering broke up. I was glad Zak and I had attended. I was feeling better after my long nap and I found I'd enjoyed singing along with the kids and roasting marshmallows I couldn't quite bring myself to eat but Scooter loved. Both he and Alex went to their cabins with their groups, so Zak and I took Charlie for a short moonlit walk along the lakeshore before turning in for the night.

"This is really nice," I said as I leaned my head on his shoulder while we strolled hand in hand. "I feel better than I have in weeks."

"Maybe you just needed a nap."

"Yeah, maybe. I'll admit trying to keep my secret was stressing me out. I'm glad the cat's out of the bag. Or maybe I should say the baby's out of the bag."

Zak kissed me on the top of the head. "I've been thinking about the nursery. I know things are pretty crazy this summer with Levi, Ellie, and Eli living with us during the remodel of the boathouse. And with everything that's going on with the construction at Zimmerman Academy, the last thing we need is another construction project…"

"And don't forget the expansion at the Zoo."

Zak stopped walking. "There's an expansion at the Zoo?"

"I guess I forgot to mention it. We talked a while back about expanding to accommodate more bears."

"I remember."

"We're already in a space crunch this summer, so I told Jeremy to go ahead and get started. I hope that's okay."

Zak put his arm around my shoulders. "Of course it's okay. The more wildlife we can rehabilitate the better. Did he find a contractor who can start right away?"

"It seems Jeremy has a friend. Anyway, you were saying something about the nursery?"

"I'm thinking we should consider remodeling our suite. We can add a door on the wall that separates the seating area from the little room we set up as a nursery for Harper."

I smiled fondly when I remembered how sweet Zak had been to surprise me with a nursery for her when my baby sister was born. We weren't even married yet then.

"Harper is older now, so there shouldn't be a problem remodeling one of the guest rooms down the hall near Alex's room for her when we babysit," Zak continued. "If we connected the two rooms with a door it would be easy to use the seating area we already have for nursing and spending quiet time with Catherine."

I hugged Zak's arm. "I love that idea. It sounds like you've been thinking about this for a while."

"I've been thinking about it since before you were pregnant. I can't wait to hold my little girl. I hope she looks like you."

"Minus the frizzy hair," I qualified.

Zak stopped walking and caressed my cheek with a finger. "I think I'm going to have to have the whole package. Of course, if Catherine ends up with my blond hair I'll love her just as much, but I can't help thinking a mini you would be just about perfect."

I stood on tiptoe and kissed him on the lips before we continued down the beach. "Catherine Dunphy had long dark hair and bright blue eyes. Ever since she told me I'd have a daughter named Catherine I've envisioned a little girl who would look like her aristocratic ancestor. I can't wait to introduce them."

It was dark and I couldn't see Zak's face clearly, but I sensed furrowed brows. "*Introduce* them?"

"I want to take Catherine—and Alex and Scooter, and maybe even Levi, Ellie, and Eli, and possibly my parents, sister, and Grandpa—to Ireland next summer. I'd like to have Catherine christened in the castle."

"Have you talked to Lord Dunphy about your idea?"

"No," I admitted. "But I did find his hidden jewels and save the castle from the developers who wanted to tear it down, so I think he owes me. Besides, if Catherine is my ancestor—and I feel certain she is— Lord Dunphy and I are related in some many-generations-removed manner."

Zak squeezed my hand. "Okay. If that's what you want that's what we'll do. We'll need to get a head count in advance so I can figure out if we'll need to charter a larger jet. Coop," Zak said, referring to the pilot he usually hired, "can fit sixteen."

"Sixteen should work, but we can discuss it at length when it gets a little closer." I paused and looked across the lake. "Is that Gordy and Polly?"

The couple appeared as little more than a silhouette in the darkness of the night, but it was clear they were kissing, and quite passionately at that.

"I don't think so," Zak said. "Gordy isn't that tall. I think it's Seth. Or possibly Felix."

Zak was right. Gordy was maybe five foot ten and Darrell was even shorter. Fred the janitor was maybe six foot tall, but I couldn't picture him necking under the moonlight, and it seemed as if the taller of the two figures was six foot at least based on the difference in height between the two people. Of course, it was dark and the figures were standing all the way across the lake. I supposed it was possible the taller of the two could look so much bigger than his companion if he was standing on an incline.

"Do you think it's Seth and Gina?" I asked. I wasn't sure knowing their identities was any of my business, but I was intrigued.

"No. Gina has short hair. That woman has long hair. You can see it blowing in the breeze. It could be Susan, or maybe the brunette who arrived later in the day yesterday. I think her name is Kelly."

Zak was right; Gina did have short hair. I continued to watch until the couple turned away from us and walked into the woods. I hoped they had a flashlight because it was pretty darn dark once you were under the canopy of the trees. Though based on the intimacy of the embrace we'd witnessed, darker was probably better for the activity I was certain they had planned.

"Now that the show is over are you ready to head back?" Zak asked.

"I am." I stood on tiptoe and kissed his neck. "And may I repeat I'm feeling a lot better than I have been."

Zak grinned. "Better enough?"

"Better enough."

Chapter 7

Friday, May 26

The sun shining in through the small slit in the closed curtains woke me the following morning. Both Zak and Charlie were gone and there wasn't a clock in the room, so I had no idea what time it was, but I found I was more rested and alert than I'd been in a long time. I lay perfectly still, waiting for the early morning nausea to grip my body as it had almost every day for the past six weeks, but so far, I felt not only well rested but hungry and not in the least nauseated.

I slowly sat up and waited to see if the familiar but unwanted queasiness would arrive. It didn't. I got up and gathered the shorts and other clothing I would wear that day. I dressed quickly, then took my toiletry bag and headed for the bathroom just down the dirt path past several campers' cabins. I used the facilities and washed up, then headed back to the cabin, where I hoped to find at least one of the chocolate doughnuts remained. I was digging through my chocolate stash, trying to put together a well-balanced meal of doughnuts, cookies, and M&M's when I heard two women talking as they passed my open window.

"No one knows what happened. It looks like she just walked off the ledge."

I abandoned my search for the chocolate fix Catherine was demanding and scooted closer to the window. The woman who was speaking—I now realized it was Polly—continued. "It was dark last night and there are those shrubs that line the edge of the ravine, so I guess it's possible she just had a few too many drinks and didn't realize where she was walking."

I put my ear close to the window but couldn't hear what was said next because the women had moved too far down the trail. The woman Polly was speaking to was one of the parent volunteers whose name I didn't remember, but as I let the content of the conversation sink in I realized the pattern of the accident every two years had continued and Mrs. Potter's death was most likely something else entirely.

I needed to find Zak, but I had no idea where he was. I grabbed my cell and dialed his number. He didn't answer, so I left a message and headed to the lake. If a body had been found dead at the bottom of a ravine there would be emergency people everywhere.

When I arrived I saw there were a lot of people standing around on the south end of the lake where Zak and I had been the previous evening when we'd seen the couple kissing on the opposite side of the small body of water. There were multiple emergency vehicles with flashing red lights in the parking area. I didn't see Zak, but I spotted Gordy and went in his direction.

"What happened?" I asked.

"You didn't hear?"

"I slept in."

"Susan Kellogg was found dead at the bottom of the ravine."

I had to wonder if she was the female half of last night's kissing couple. Zak and I had speculated it could be her because of her long hair. If so, then who was the man she was with? Seth?

"Did it happen this morning or last night?" I asked.

"Her body was found about thirty minutes ago. She hasn't been seen since last night. She was pretty wasted and everyone thought she was going back to her cabin after the campfire, but apparently she must have decided to go for a walk."

"So the girls in her cabin never saw her come in?"

Gordy shook his head. "I haven't spoken to any of her girls personally, but it seems no one knew she was missing until this morning. I hate to say it, but the way things unfolded feels eerily like what happened when Cleo died."

Yes, I thought, it did.

"Did you know Cleo wasn't the first person to die at the camp?" I asked Gordy.

Gordy raised his brows. "There was talk of someone who drowned, although I don't know all the details."

"Her name was Sarah Collins and she drowned in the lake in the middle of the night. Like Cleo and Susan, it appeared as if she took a late-night stroll and somehow ended up dead. Her death was considered nothing more than a terrible accident and there wasn't a thorough investigation."

Gordy glanced at me. "It sounds as if you don't think it was an accident."

"Could it have been? I mean, think about it. What are the odds that three young women would have strange accidents all within a six-year time frame?"

Gordy didn't answer, but I could see he was taking my comment seriously. He glanced at the area the emergency personnel had taped off. "So you think Cleo was murdered as well?"

I took a deep breath before I answered. "I wasn't here and I don't have all the details. Like I said, I think it's odd that now four women have suffered extremely unfortunate accidents within six years. How could it be just chance? They died in different ways; three died while supposedly alone late at night, while Wilma died during the day with people around her. Her death seemed to have broken a pattern, but only if the pattern is set by time of death and not something else."

"Like what?"

I tilted my head to the side. "I don't know. Not yet at least." I looked around. "Have you seen Zak?"

"He was talking to one of the cops earlier. It seemed as if he knew him."

"Must have been Officer Michaelson. Zak spoke to him after I found Mrs. Potter's body."

"That's right," Gordy said. "You were the one who found her body in the pantry. I heard you had blood all over your hands."

"I didn't kill her, if that's what you're suggesting. I tried to save her, but it was too late. For a while I thought her death had something to do with the two-year pattern, but now I'm pretty sure it didn't. Is there anything about Susan's death that stands out to you as being similar to Cleo and Wilma's?"

"What do you mean, similar?"

"Is there anyone all three women didn't get along with, or maybe someone they all did get along with in an intimate way?"

"Now you're the one who seems to be suggesting something. Do you think *I* did it?"

I looked directly at Gordy. "Did you?"

"Of course not. Geez. Is that why you were asking me about the women I'd been with yesterday?"

"Actually it was. And yes, I did suspect you for a while, but not so much now. There are only a handful of people who've been here for all four deaths, at least as far as I know. If they're all related the pool of suspects is narrowed significantly. As far as I know, Gina, Seth, and Fred are the only people who have been on staff here for the entire time."

"You think one of them did it?"

"I don't know. Maybe." I watched as a covered stretcher carried by two rescue workers was slipped into the back of an ambulance. One of the uniformed officers stopped to say something to Gina, who was standing next to Seth. A few minutes later another uniformed officer came out of the administration office. He was followed by Zak, who looked very unhappy. He glanced in my direction and shrugged.

I remembered Susan had been with a tall man last night. Zak was tall, pretty much taller than anyone else at the camp. It occurred to me that someone else had seem Susan with a tall man and told the cops about it. My instinct was to go to him immediately, but my Zodar told me to wait.

"I suppose it could be someone from town," Gordy eventually said. "There are always a few townies sniffing around the female counselors. A couple I can think of have been showing up here for years."

"Are visitors allowed on the premises late at night?"

"No, but that doesn't stop them from coming in through the woods. Wouldn't surprise me a bit to find out Susan had hooked up with a townie. She didn't seem to give the rest of us here at the lake the time of day."

A few minutes later Officer Michaelson came across the lawn to me. "Mrs. Zimmerman, we have a few questions for you and your husband if you'd be so kind as to come with me."

"I'd be happy to speak to you, but before I go I need to know where my kids and my dog are."

"Mr. Zimmerman had a dog with him this morning when we first arrived. When I told him I needed to speak to him, he called a girl he introduced me to as Alex to come get him. I believe the girl and the dog are waiting in Gina's office."

"I need to see them and then I'll come with you and tell you everything I know. Do you think it will be okay if we drive our own vehicle?"

"That should be fine. I'll follow you into town."

******

For the third time since Zak and I had been at the camp I found myself sitting in an interrogation room in the small Duck Lake Police Station. Given the circumstances, I supposed I could understand why the police would be interested in speaking to us, but I hated that we'd spent very little time as a family on our first family vacation of the summer.

"Seems like you're becoming regular visitors to our little establishment," Detective Swanson, the man who had interviewed me on that first day, said.

Zak was in another room, talking to someone else. I wished the police could have interviewed us together, but I knew why they hadn't.

"I don't know what anyone told you, but Zak didn't kill Susan," I insisted. "We were together the entire evening."

The detective narrowed his eyes. "It's interesting you would jump right in with that when I haven't said a word about your husband being a suspect."

"I figured that was why he was here. Why *we're* here. The man with Susan last night was tall and Zak is tall, so I just figured..." I stopped rambling and took a minute to gather my thoughts. "I'm making it worse, aren't I?"

Detective Swanson actually chuckled. "Yes, you are. But not to worry. I had a long chat with your Sheriff Salinger in Ashton Falls and he was willing to personally vouch for both of you. You are, however, considered to be witnesses if we later determine the couple you saw across the lake did include Susan Kellogg."

I let out a breath. "Okay; good. What do you want to know?"

"I understand there was a campfire last night and all the campers as well as the entire staff attended."

"Yes. That's correct."

"Do you specifically remember seeing Ms. Kellogg there?"

"I do. She was supervising the girls who were staying in the cabin she was assigned to."

"And did she interact with anyone else during the event?"

"Yes. Everyone was chatting with everyone else. I wasn't specifically focused on Susan, but it was a fun and lively affair, so I'm sure she spoke to a lot of people."

"Was there anyone at the campfire who wasn't in some way associated with the camp?"

I considered the question. "No. Not that I noticed anyway."

"I'm waiting for the tox screen for confirmation, but one of the other counselors I spoke to said Ms. Kellogg was intoxicated during the campfire. Do you remember if she was acting oddly?"

I paused and thought about it. "No. I don't think so. I mean, I don't remember thinking 'Geez, that girl is wasted.'"

"Okay; tell me about the couple you saw by the lake after the campfire."

"Zak and I were taking a walk along the lakeshore and we saw a couple locked in a passionate embrace. It was dark, so all we really saw was the silhouette of the couple. The man was tall and the woman had long hair. We knew that because the woman's hair was blowing in the breeze. We suspected the woman could be Susan, but we didn't know that for certain."

"And the man?"

I hesitated. I didn't want to begin tossing names around based on nothing more than a hunch.

"Ms. Zimmerman, did you and your husband speculate as to who the male participant may have been?"

"Based on height and height alone, we suspected it could be a counselor named Seth Greenway."

"That's interesting. It was Seth Greenway who gave me your husband's name. He said he saw Susan with a tall man he suspected could have been him."

"Well, it wasn't. First of all, Zak would never in a million years cheat on me. And secondly, I already told you Zak was with me the entire evening."

"Can you verify his whereabouts at two a.m.?"

"Two a.m.? Why that specific time?"

"It's the estimated time of death."

That was quite a while after Zak and I saw the couple at the lake.

"Is there a problem?" Detective Swanson asked.

I shook my head. "No. Not a problem exactly. It's just that Zak and I saw the couple at around midnight. They headed into the woods and we went to our cabin. I suppose if Susan fell after the couple had…well, been intimate, it's reasonable she could have been alone, but it's also possible the male half of the couple would have walked her back to her cabin. Unless, of course, she didn't fall and he pushed her."

The detective looked directly at me. "You still haven't answered my question regarding your husband's whereabouts at two a.m."

"We were in our cabin asleep at two a.m."

"So you can't vouch for the fact that he was actually there?"

"Okay, look: Yes, I was asleep at two a.m., so no, I can't say I know beyond a shadow of a doubt that Zak was in the cabin with me, but this line of questioning is a waste of time. I didn't kill Mrs. Potter. Zak didn't kill Susan. But there's someone out there killing people and it would behoove us to focus on that."

The detective sat back. "So you do believe Ms. Kellogg was pushed from the ledge."

"Of course I do," I said in a voice so loud as to be considered a scream. "Hers is the fourth supposedly accidental death in six years. It would be too bizarre if these deaths turned out to be accidents, as the people in your office would like everyone to believe."

"I agree," Detective Swanson responded.

"You do?"

"I only transferred to Duck Lake a year ago, so I wasn't around when the other women died, but your theory that the deaths were related piqued my interest and I pulled all three files. While I understand why the investigating officer came to the conclusion he did, I can also see how you might determine there was more going on. With the death of Ms. Kellogg, I'm even more inclined to embrace your theory, although the other three deaths occurred at the end of the season and Ms. Kellogg died after only two days. Still, it does seem she may be linked to the others. But if all four deaths are linked, who's the killer? It would have to be someone who was around the entire time. Additionally, I have to wonder if Mrs. Potter's death is also linked."

I entwined my fingers and set my hands on the table in front of me. "I've also considered that. She didn't fit the profile of the first three, so I never considered her to be the fourth accident victim, but what if she knew or overheard something about what had occurred? It seems like the killer might have had reason to silence her. I understand she called 911 prior to her death. Have you listened to the recording of the call?"

Detective Swanson nodded. "Unfortunately, she called from her cell and the reception was spotty. The 911 operator could make out the location from which the call originated, so emergency personnel were sent to investigate. Other than that, there were only a few words that were recognizable, and they exist in isolation."

"What did she say?"

"After the operator answered there was at least fifteen seconds of static. During that time all you can hear on the tape is the operator asking if there's an emergency and trying to get information. Eventually, you can hear a woman say, 'Duck Lake.' That's followed by static, and then you hear the words *skunk* and *attack*."

"Mrs. Potter said she was being attacked by a skunk?"

"No, I don't think so. There was static between the words, so, as I said, I imagine they were taken out of context. The only other words we were able to define were *cereal* and *beans*."

"Okay, that's not a lot, but at some point the words could start to make sense. What else do you know about Mrs. Potter's death?"

"Other than the fact that you're the main and really only suspect, not a lot. I don't suppose you've come up with anything? Sheriff Salinger told me about your record for solving the murders you investigate. It's quite impressive."

"Thank you, and no, I don't have much at this point. I do have reason to suspect the camp administrator, Gina Keebler, might be up to something, but I don't have enough to point a finger. I believe if you allow Zak and me to take a look at the police reports for Sarah Collins, Cleo Thornton, and Wilma Partridge, we might be able to help you develop a list of viable suspects at the very least."

Detective Swanson drummed his fingers on the table. I assumed he was considering my request. After a full minute, he finally spoke. "Okay. But you look at the files here, with an officer in attendance, and you agree that any information in the files is to be considered confidential."

"Agreed. I never had breakfast, so would it be asking too much to have some sandwiches brought in?"

Chapter 8

Officer Michaelson brought Zak into the room where I'd been interviewed. He took our lunch order, then returned to the main lobby, where he sent the receptionist out for our sandwiches before pulling the files we'd requested, as well as yellow legal pads and pens with which we could make notes. Then he sat down across from us and waited.

Unlike the notes we'd found at the newspaper the day before, the police reports included a lot of graphic details, including photographs of the dead women. I felt the familiar churning in my stomach, so I quickly looked past the photos and focused on the text. A lot of the material was things we'd already learned, so my point was to identify anything new that could provide the link we needed.

"It says here that Sarah Collins drowned in the lake and her body wasn't discovered until the next morning, but it doesn't say who discovered her or what time that was," I said, looking across the table at Officer Michaelson.

He frowned. "Let me take a look."

I passed him the report, which stated that Sarah had been at the campfire but had left early to go to her cabin. Her cabinmates had all reported that she wasn't there when they arrived, but they didn't know where she'd gone. It was speculated that she'd really left the fire to hook up with one of the other counselors, but the investigator discovered that the counselor everyone thought she'd gone to meet was with two other friends the entire evening.

"That's odd. The body must have been found early in the morning, when everyone began to leave their cabins for breakfast, but there isn't any mention of who exactly found it. Let me check the computer report to see if I can find any additional information."

"And while you're at it, the names of the friends who provided the alibi were given, but I didn't see the name of the counselor Sarah was thought to have hooked up with in the first place. I think that might be useful information."

Officer Michaelson stood up. "I'll see what I can find and be right back."

After he left Zak turned to me. "Did you notice anything odd about the photos of the dead women?"

"I didn't really look at them. Did you find something?"

Zak took out a photo of each woman and laid them side by side. I bit down on my lip to suppress the nausea that was threatening. "What am I looking at?"

"Their wrists."

I made myself look at the photos. Sarah, Cleo, and Wilma each had a beaded bracelet on her wrist. They were all slightly different but all appeared to be homemade, of jet-black beads of varying shapes with one white bead in the center. It made sense they would have been wearing the bracelet if they'd made the jewelry the day they died. Sure, they could have made the bracelets on a previous day, but at least one of them probably would have taken hers off for one reason or another. The other thing to remember was that they were all counselors. Did counselors as a rule participate in the arts and crafts projects?

I wasn't certain, but I supposed it would be easy enough to find out.

"Did Susan have a beaded bracelet on her wrist when her body was found?" I asked Zak.

"I don't know, but I think we should ask."

"Susan was in charge of the crafts yesterday. They made picture frames. I know because I joined her group. If she had a bracelet on it wouldn't be because she'd just made it that day."

Zak made a note on his pad. "I'll ask when Officer Michaelson gets back."

We went back to our files. The bracelets might not mean anything, but they did seem to provide a link between the three dead women. The more links we uncovered, the better chance we had of making a case to the police that the deaths were murders and further investigation should be initiated.

The next file I looked at was that of Cleo Thornton. There was a note indicating that the medical examiner had determined she'd died from blunt force trauma to the head, but the ME's actual report wasn't there. Come to think of it, I didn't remember seeing an ME report in Sarah's file either. I'd need to ask about that.

The police report indicated that the body had been discovered in a heavily wooded area at least eight hours after she'd died. The head wound was on the right temple and there was a large bolder near the body that was covered with blood, seeming to indicate that Cleo was walking through the dark forest, tripped on the log that was near her feet, and hit her head, eventually bleeding to death. I decided to risk a bout with nausea to look more closely at the photos taken at the scene. The log Cleo supposedly tripped over was fairly large, although not so much so that tripping would have been an impossibility. Cleo had been wearing shorts, a sweatshirt, and flip-flops when her body was found. It seemed to me if she'd really tripped, her shins, ankles, and feet would have been skinned from the log's rough bark. The fact that she'd skinned her legs might not have seemed important enough to mention in the report, but I'd be interested in finding out about it. The photo in the report showed Cleo laying on her stomach, where she fell, and any abrasions would have been on the front of her legs.

"Did you come across a photo of the front of Cleo's legs?" I asked Zak.

"Yeah. Right here." He handed it to me.

Cleo's feet were pretty torn up and there were scratches on her legs, but she could have received those from walking through the woods in nothing but flip-flops. If she hit the log with the front of her shin while walking and then fell over it, there should have been obvious scrape marks, but based on this photo it was hard to say if that was what had occurred. What I found interesting now was that Cleo's hand was clenched in the first photo I'd seen, showing her as she'd appeared when she was found. If you found yourself falling wouldn't you try to catch yourself with your hands? And if that happened, wouldn't your hands be open?

I pushed the photo in front of Zak. "Look at Cleo's hand. Doesn't it look like she's clutching something?"

Zak picked the photo up and studied it. "Yeah. It does look that way. Did you notice if the report says they found anything in her hand?"

"No. But I'll keep looking."

I supposed a clenched hand could be an effect of rigor mortis setting in, but my Zodar was whispering that there could be something more to it.

When Officer Michaelson returned with our sandwiches and bottled water Zak and I took a break to eat while he filled us in on what he'd discovered in the computer database.

"The person who found Sarah Collins's body was a minor, which is why the name was left off the report. I did some additional digging; it appears the camper left his cabin early that morning to get some towels from the bathroom and saw something floating in the lake. The something turned out to be the body. The camper ran back to tell his counselor, who called the police."

"Who was the counselor he told?" I asked.

"Seth Greenway."

Interesting.

"And why was he sent for towels?" Zak asked.

"It seems Seth was goofing around with some of the kids and one of them hit his head and it started to bleed."

"He hit his head and it bled? It seems as if he needed more than some towels. Why wasn't the camper taken to the infirmary?"

"I'm not sure," Officer Michaelson admitted. "Maybe it wasn't all that bad. Head wounds, even minor ones, have a tendency to bleed quite a lot."

Okay, so Seth sent a kid to get towels and the kid found the body. I wondered if

Seth knew about the body and intentionally created the need to send a kid on an errand so he'd be the one to call 911, thereby removing himself as a suspect. It did seem Seth's name was coming up a lot as we dug deeper into the deaths.

"Did the report in the database give you the name of the counselor Sarah was supposedly meeting the night she died?"

"It was Rich Tidwell, and we'd already determined he was with his friends the entire evening."

Or at least that was his story.

"We have another question about Susan Kellogg's death," Zak spoke up. "Was she wearing jewelry of any sort when her body was found?"

Michaelson paused. "I'm not sure. Is it important? I can probably find out."

"We think it might be important," Zak said. "If you can check while we finish eating we'll fill you in once we have the answer."

"Okay. I'll be back in a minute."

I glanced at Zak after Michaelson left the room. "Do you think Seth could be our guy?"

"Maybe. His name is coming up a lot."

"Alex took a ton of photos last night. I wonder if she got one of Susan. If she did we can see if she was wearing any jewelry and compare it to what Officer Michaelson finds."

"Text her to ask," Zak suggested.

I did, and we finished our meal in anticipation of returning to the reports. As I ate, I wondered if there was any other way to find out if Cleo was clutching something in her hand when her body was found.

"Do you know if the same ME investigated all three deaths?" I asked Zak.

He picked up the reports and looked through them. "Spencer Cook investigated all three deaths. Why do you ask?"

I shrugged. "There are some notes referring to an ME report, but the report itself isn't included in any of the files. It seems to me there may be additional information included in those reports that could be helpful. I wonder if the same ME is in charge of Susan's death as well."

"We can check with Officer Michaelson when he returns."

"What I'd really like to do is speak to the ME. Getting a look at the original reports could be helpful, but a face-to-face conversation would be better."

Michaelson came back a few minutes later. "Susan Kellogg was wearing a beaded bracelet on her left wrist when her body was found."

Bingo; we had found our link.

Zak showed Michaelson the photos of the other women, pointing out the similar bracelets they all wore. Meanwhile I texted back and forth with Alex as she sent me some photos from the previous evening one at a time. There was one of Susan that clearly showed her left wrist free of any adornment. The bracelet, I thought, must have been put on her wrist after she left the campfire. Was our killer a gentleman who plied his victims with handmade gifts before killing them? It seemed so, although, to be fair, we didn't know with a certainty that the killer was a man.

"I know the bracelets seem like a clue, but the kids make them every year, and one or more of the campers make them for their counselors. You'll see what I mean when the kids have bracelet day this year," Officer Michaelson informed us.

Darn. I'd really thought we had something here.

"Can you tell me the name of the ME looking at Susan Kellogg's remains?" I asked.

"Spencer Cook. He's been the ME in this area for decades."

"I'd be interested in speaking to him. Do you think you can set it up?"

"I'm not sure it would be appropriate to ask the ME to discuss sensitive, confidential information with a civilian. I hope you understand," Michaelson said.

******

Zak and I sat in the car talking after we'd left the police station. We hadn't found out a lot more, other than the fact that Mrs. Potter's 911 call was, indeed, garbled to the point of being useless.

"Do you think you would be able to clean up the background static?" I asked my genius of a husband.

"Maybe, but not with the equipment I have here," Zak answered.

"What about Pi?" I asked, referring to Zak's ward, who was in college but due to come home soon for the summer.

"Yeah, he could do it, but we'd need to have a copy of the original recording sent to him. He'll be in Ashton Falls later today, so if we can get our hands on the recording he could work on it this evening."

"Maybe we should talk to Detective Swanson. He seemed to welcome our help. And while we're at it, we can ask him about a meeting with the ME. I know Michaelson didn't think it would be appropriate, but it couldn't hurt to ask."

"Do you have Detective Swanson's direct number?"

I held up a business card. "He gave it to me that first day in case I remembered something important."

Zak shrugged. "It wouldn't hurt to ask."

I called Detective Swanson, who answered, and made my requests. Once he realized my Zak Zimmerman was *the* Zak Zimmerman of Zimmerman Software, he agreed to forward the 911 call to Pi. Additionally, he said he'd speak to the ME, then call me back to let me know if he had time to speak to us today. I hung up the phone and looked at Zak. Something had occurred to me as I'd been speaking with the detective. "I wonder, if a single person is killing these women, why the pattern was altered with Wilma Partridge."

"Are you referring to the time of day when her death took place?"

"I am. Gordy mentioned that as well when I spoke to him. Sarah, Cleo, and Susan were all killed at around two a.m. In all three cases they appeared to have been outside alone when they should have been sleeping. All three bodies were found the next morning. And all three were involved in a relationship of some sort. It's been suggested Sarah was seeing a counselor named Rich Tidwell, Gordy admitted to having been having a summer fling with Cleo, and assuming it was Susan we saw last night, she apparently was hooking up with someone. When I asked Gordy about Wilma he said she was a tight ass who wouldn't be interested in anything he was offering. He said it in such a way as to indicate it was unlikely she would have been interested in hooking up with anyone at the camp. She also died during the day, with a group of witnesses nearby, which further broke the pattern."

"I suppose finding out why her death was different could provide a clue, though I have no idea where to start."

"Seth," I said. "Susan told me that Wilma wasn't a good rider, so Gina never assigned her to the horses. I suggested someone might have gotten sick at the last minute and Wilma was asked to fill in, and Susan's response was that Gina still would have switched things around to avoid having Wilma take a group horseback riding. I asked Susan who would have made the switch if Gina hadn't been around and she said Seth most likely would have done it. We both see things coming back to Seth. What if Gina was away and Seth intentionally assigned Wilma to the horses? Susan also said Darrell's group had made slingshots that week. What if Seth was hiding in the woods and used one of those to fire a rock or some other hard object at Wilma's horse to make him bolt."

"That's a lot of *what if*s, but you do have a good theory there," Zak admitted. "But if Seth is the person we're looking for I don't think asking him about it before we find some sort of proof is the best way to go."

"Okay. How do we get proof?"

Zak looked out the windshield at the forest before us. "I don't know exactly; I guess we just keep investigating." He turned to me. "I'm worried about conducting an investigation at a somewhat remote camp while accompanied by two children and a pregnant wife. Maybe we should take more of a backseat and leave the actual frontline work to the cops. At this point they seem to be working with us."

I would never forgive myself if something happened to Scooter, Alex, or Catherine. "Okay. I agree. But we'll need to be careful not to let anyone know we're working with the cops. There's no reason anyone other than Detective Swanson needs to know Pi is working on the 911 tape and we don't need to mention our conversation with the ME should we get in to see him. Of course, if we're allowed to speak to him, we won't be able to do our shifts this afternoon."

"I'll call Gina and tell her we're still tied up at the police station," Zak offered. "That should get us freed up for the rest of the day at least."

I called Alex to see how she was doing, but when she didn't answer I left a message. I tried Scooter, who didn't answer either, but he rarely carried his phone. I left him a message anyway, just in case he thought to check. Zak was still on the phone with Gina, so I took a minute to gather my thoughts.

On one hand, I felt invigorated by the fact that we seemed to be making some progress. On the other, despite my assurances to Zak and my declaration to the contrary, I wondered if we weren't making a mistake by staying. Maybe Zak had been right from the beginning and we should have taken the kids and headed home.

Initially, we'd stayed because Detective Swanson had told me that I had to because I was the prime suspect in Mrs. Potter's death. Based on the events of the afternoon, I assumed that was no longer true. I'd always had an inner need to solve the murders in which I'd become involved, but even I had to admit I'd put myself in danger on more than one occasion. Before, when it was just my life involved, I wasn't overly concerned about the risk inherent in tracking down a killer, but now I had Catherine to think about.

I put my hand on my stomach. I couldn't wait to feel her kick. I'd pictured her a hundred times in my mind and now that her existence had become a reality I couldn't wait for her to arrive. Yet as excited as I was, I was just as terrified. Sure, I was already a mother to Alex and Scooter, but they'd come to me as ten-year-olds; Catherine would be a totally helpless newborn. Would I know what to do to keep her healthy and happy? Would I be able to comfort her and make her feel safe and secure in a world that wasn't always that way? How did other new mothers deal with all the anxiety?

My phone rang, interrupting my mental breakdown. "We have the okay to speak to the ME," I said to Zak after speaking to Detective Swanson. "He's expecting us."

******

The medical examiner's office was located in the larger town of Bryton Lake, a fifteen-minute drive from Duck Lake. Bryton Lake was the county seat in an area surrounded by tiny towns and farming communities, offering centralized services to the whole county. As soon as we arrived at the county building we were shown to Dr. Cook's office.

"Mr. and Mrs. Zimmerman, please have a seat," he indicated.

"Thank you for agreeing to speak to us," Zak jumped in.

"Detective Swanson informed me that you're interested in gaining additional information about the series of deaths that have taken place at Duck Lake."

"Yes, that's correct," Zak answered.

"I don't know what I can tell you that wasn't included in my reports, but feel free to ask and I'll answer if I can."

I decided it was my turn to speak up. "It was determined that Cleo Thornton died as a result of tripping over a log and hitting her head on a rock. In the photos taken of her at the scene of the accident, the injury to her legs doesn't seem consistent with the specific log she was found lying in front of."

"That's a good observation from someone who isn't a professional," Dr.

Cook commented. "And you're correct. There were no wounds on Ms. Thornton's body to suggest she'd fallen over a log. She had a significant amount of alcohol in her system that would have caused her to become drowsy and disoriented, so it's possible she became dizzy and fell to the ground, hitting her head when she did so."

"Is it possible she was pushed and tripping was never part of the equation?" I asked.

"Yes. That's a possibility."

I glanced at Zak, who seemed content to listen as I continued. "I spoke to the counselor Cleo was involved with that summer. He said she was going to meet him at the lake at midnight but never showed up. Can you tell me if Cleo had engaged in sexual activity on the night of her death?"

"She had."

Interesting. I wondered if Cleo had another guy on the side. Just because Gordy claimed to be faithful to his summer flings didn't mean his women didn't cheat. Of course, she could also have been attacked on her way to the lake.

"Did it appear the sex was consensual?"

"There were no indications it wasn't."

So if Cleo was cheating who was she cheating with?

"In the photo taken at the site of her death Cleo's hand was clenched. It almost looked as if she was hanging on to something. Did you find something in her hand?"

"No. There was nothing in her hand when she was brought in. It's possible the police officers who responded to the scene removed the object if there had ever been one, but that wasn't disclosed to me."

I paused to consider my next question. "Let's talk about the other two women: Sarah Collins and Wilma Partridge. During your investigations did you find anything odd about their deaths?"

"Wilma Partridge fell from a horse and broke her neck. There was never any question that that's what happened; there were ten witnesses who all agreed on the series of events leading to her death. Because the death occurred by accident I wasn't called in to look at the body and wasn't involved in the investigation in any way."

"And Sarah Collins?"

"Sarah Collins drowned. There was a large quantity of alcohol in her system. There wasn't evidence of any defensive wounds on the body so, like Wilma Partridge, her death was determined to be an accident after only a cursory investigation."

"Did you look at the body at all?"

"I did a tox screen, but a full autopsy wasn't requested."

"And Susan Kellogg?" I asked.

"I haven't had the opportunity to look at the body yet, but I believe a full autopsy will be requested given the nature of her death and the reports by yourself and Seth Greenway that she was seen with a man prior to her death. And given the recent murder of the cook, Betty Potter, there's reason to consider that her fall from the ravine may have resulted from being pushed or thrown. I should know more once I've had the chance to autopsy the victim."

"Will you do that today?" I asked.

"If the paperwork comes through in time. Now, if there isn't anything else, I do have a busy day."

"I just have one more question relating to Mrs. Potter."

"Detective Swanson only asked me to share my results for Sarah Collins, Cleo Thornton, and Wilma Partridge with you. He didn't mention Betty Potter. If you'd like information on Mrs. Potter's death you'll need to speak to Detective Swanson to obtain his authorization. I'd be surprised if he agreed to share information because her death is part of an active investigation."

"I understand." I stood up, preparing to leave. "Thank you for your time."

Chapter 9

It seemed more and more likely that the deaths of Sarah Collins, Cleo Thornton, Wilma Partridge, and Susan Kellogg weren't related to Mrs. Potter's. I'd initially set out to find Mrs. Potter's killer and by now I was beginning to wonder if looking in to the deaths of the four young women had been nothing more than a distraction. And yet …

"Do you find it odd that Susan's death happened when it did?" I asked to Zak as we drove back to Duke Lake.

"What do you mean?"

"Sarah, Cleo, and Wilma all died during the last week of camp, but Susan died at the very beginning of the season. The entire staff hasn't even arrived yet. I feel like her death had broken the pattern, if there is one."

"Maybe Mrs. Potter's death caused the killer to act sooner than usual," Zak speculated.

"Perhaps. But if that's the case it would seem Mrs. Potter had to have been killed by the same person who killed the others, and I was beginning to think otherwise."

Zak turned off the highway onto a county road. "Keep in mind that we don't know for certain the others were murdered. The deaths do look as if they could have been accidents after all. It's more of just a hunch on our part that they were aided by another person."

"I guess that's true. Do we have time to stop by the newspaper to take another look? We never did find the notes from Sarah's death. Maybe someone said something to Burt's grandfather that will lead to a clue."

"Yeah, we have time. I don't think Gina scheduled us for any group activities today, although I did tell her we'd be back in time to help with dinner and the campfire."

"I want to stop by the little store when we're in town too. Catherine and I ate all the doughnuts and most of the cookies we bought yesterday."

Zak glanced at me out of the corner of his eye. "Are you sure you should be eating all that chocolate?"

"Probably not, but I've been feeling so much better since I went on that chocolate binge. I figured it won't kill me to give into my cravings at least until I get home. Besides, all the stress from investigating is making me hungry."

"Well, at least try to eat something healthy with the chocolate. Expectant moms need a lot of vitamins to nourish their growing baby."

"Chocolate has vitamins," I argued.

Zak snorted.

"But I know I need a full range of vitamins and I'll try to eat a balanced diet," I added.

Burt was on the phone when we arrived at the newspaper office, but he motioned for us to sit down. There was a pile of paperwork on the counter and it appeared as if he'd been working on a story. Probably something about the two recent deaths at the camp. If the paper was published twice a month there would probably be an edition coming out either at the end or the beginning of the month and another two weeks later.

"Looks like you had some more excitement out at the camp," Burt said when he hung up the phone.

"Unfortunately, we've had more than our share of excitement in the past couple of days," I acknowledged. "I imagine you've been following up on both Susan's and Mrs. Potter's deaths?"

"I have," Burt confirmed. "I took another look at the three older cases as well after you were here yesterday. At first I wasn't all that certain there was a link, but since the most recent death I think you're on to something."

"That's why we're here. We hoped you'd let us take another look at the stuff in your storage room. We didn't have time to find everything yesterday."

"I'll do you one better. After you left yesterday I found the three boxes containing the notes from the first three counselor deaths and brought them inside. I have the notes spread out on the table in the press room. I've been going through them all morning, but you're welcome to take a look too."

I smiled. "Thank you. We'd appreciate it."

"Come on back." Burt started down the narrow hallway. "I have a fresh pot of coffee if you'd like some."

I politely declined, but Zak accepted a cup. Burt sat down on one side of the table and we took chairs across from him.

"Now that you've gone through your grandfather's notes what do you think?" I asked as I picked up the stack of paper closest to me.

"Taken in isolation, each death appears to be nothing more than a tragic accident. When you look at all three as a series of events it does seem there's something more going on, especially after the death of the fourth woman this morning. I went out to the camp a while ago to interview the director. Ms. Keebler gave me what seemed to be a rehearsed speech that I recorded so I wouldn't forget anything. It struck me as odd that she didn't seem all that emotional about the death of one of her staff members. I understand Susan Kellogg worked at the camp three years before this one; you'd think the two of them would know each other fairly well."

I nodded. "That was my understanding as well. What exactly did Gina tell you?"

"She started off by saying how grieved everyone at the camp was and then gave me Ms. Kellogg's age and hometown. She confirmed the report I'd received that the counselor died as the result of a terrible accident, and when I asked about the man she was seen with last night she told me she was involved with one of the counselors, Gordy Sinclair."

"Susan wasn't seeing Gordy," I interrupted. "Gordy is involved with Polly."

"Which is exactly what he told me when I spoke to him. He had no idea why Ms. Keebler would say that. I found it strange as well but didn't think a whole lot about it until I came back here and started going through my grandfather's notes. Ms. Keebler paired Mr. Sinclair with all three of the women who've died."

"All three?" I said. "Gordy's only been working at the camp for four summers before this one."

"That's what he told me too, but apparently he worked here in town the summer the first woman died. Or at least that's what Ms. Keebler told me. I haven't had a chance to confirm it with Sinclair yet."

This was new information. "In town where?"

"At the burger shack on Main. According to what Ms. Keebler's told my grandfather at the time of Sarah Collins's death, she'd been dating a man from town named Gordy Sinclair at the time of her death."

I'd spoken to Gordy on two occasions and he'd never said a thing about knowing Sarah. In fact, when I'd brought up the fact that a woman had died before Cleo he'd as much as said he didn't know her and couldn't remember her name. He'd admitted to being involved with Cleo, and I remembered reading that Gina had indicated as much in her interview. She'd also claimed Gordy was involved with Wilma, but he'd flat-out denied having anything to do with her to me. And Susan? I couldn't know for a fact whether she and Gordy had something going on, but he was openly hooking up with Polly this year, and the man we'd seen last night with the woman I was now assuming was Susan was quite a bit taller than Gordy.

It seemed clear someone was lying, but who, and why?

"What else did Gina say?"

"Not a lot. She was impatient and I could tell she just wanted to get the interview over with. She assured me that while Ms. Kellogg's accident was tragic, the camp would continue to hold all scheduled activities and another counselor was being brought in to take Susan's place. In the meantime, one of the female parents agreed to sleep in the cabin with the girls tonight."

"Did you happen to ask her about Mrs. Potter while you were there?"

"I did, and she declined to comment because she'd obviously been murdered and the investigation into her death was still ongoing."

While that was true, the fact that Gina seemed to be so unaffected by both deaths really bothered me. I hadn't had a chance to speak to her personally since everything had gone down, but I was going to make it a priority to track her down when Zak and I returned to the camp.

"Did you speak to anyone else while you were at the camp?" I asked when I realized I'd probably learned as much as I could from Burt about Gina's interview.

"The counselors were all busy with their campers and Ms. Keebler—rightfully so— didn't want me to speak to them with the kids listening in. I did manage to speak to the woman they brought in to replace Mrs. Potter. Her name is Judy Davidson and she lives here in Duck Lake and has, apparently, helped out in the past when Mrs. Potter was ill or needed a day off."

I sat back in my chair. "And what did Ms. Davidson have to say?"

"She indicated that as far as she knew, Mrs. Potter and Ms. Keebler didn't get along all that well and that they were involved in a lawsuit regarding a number of recipes Ms. Keebler used in a cookbook that Mrs. Potter claimed to have originally developed."

This I'd been expecting ever since I first learned that both women had published cookbooks. What I didn't know was why Mrs. Potter had returned to the camp year after year if she didn't get along with the administrator. I asked Burt if that had come up in the interview he'd had with the new cook.

"Yes, it did. Mrs. Davidson said Mrs. Potter had a multiyear contract that was signed by the administrator before Ms. Keebler and was good for another four years. Ms. Keebler couldn't fire or refuse to rehire Mrs. Potter without very specific cause, so her hands were tied. I asked Mrs. Davidson why she thought Mrs. Potter didn't just quit after the conflict with the cookbook came to light, and she said, 'Betty wasn't going to let no lyin' cheat run her off.'"

Suddenly I was wondering if Gina wasn't responsible for Mrs. Potter's death. The conversation I'd overheard in the woods had come after Mrs. Potter was dead, so the *she* the pair was referring to couldn't have been her, but perhaps it was

Susan they were discussing. It was possible she'd seen or overheard something and was threatening to tell the police what she knew. Gina knew the first three women had died under suspicious circumstances; maybe she'd copied the idea of making the death look like an accident and carried it out as soon as she could. Or maybe she was responsible for all four deaths. There was something about her that was starting to bother me.

Zak and I chatted with Burt a bit longer, but he didn't have much else I found to be of relevance. We headed to the store and then out to the camp, where I hoped to run into Gina so I could ask my own questions and develop my own opinions as to exactly how she fit into everything.

Unfortunately, not only were Gina and all the other counselors busy but the busyness of the day was beginning to catch up to me and I found I was suddenly exhausted. Zak was asked to help with a group, but I was free, so I checked in with Alex and Scooter, then took Charlie to our cabin, where I hoped the two of us could find enough quiet time to take a power nap.

******

The sound of my cell phone ringing woke me a couple of hours later. "Jeremy?" I said, answering between yawns.

"Were you sleeping?"

I sat up and leaned back against the pillows. "Charlie and I were taking a power nap, but it's time for us to wake up anyway. What's up?"

"I wanted to let you know that I managed to catch the golden retriever we've been after. She's pregnant and a bit skinny but otherwise healthy."

I let out a sigh of relief. "That's good. How does she seem?"

"She was pretty skittish at first and hated being locked up in a kennel, so I took her home. Rosalie has pretty much adopted her and she's good with Morgan too, so unless an owner turns up I think I'm going to keep her." Rosalie was Jeremy's nine-year-old stepdaughter, Morgan his three-year-old daughter.

"That's great. I'm glad our girl found a home. We should post all the usual notices, though, just to be sure there isn't someone looking for her."

"I have, and I made sure Rosalie understood that if we found her owner we'd have to give her back. She's a bright kid and has had to deal with a lot in the past, so my sense is that she's tough enough to do the right thing should it come to it."

I was happy Jeremy was taking a special interest in the golden, especially because she was pregnant, but I hoped Rosalie didn't end up getting hurt. I'd had my own experiences with bringing home a pregnant stray only to have the owner show up two months later after I'd become attached to both the dog and her puppies.

"Did you get started on the bear cage?" I asked.

"My friend came in today, took measurements, and ordered all the materials he'll need. He's starting on Monday."

"Monday is Memorial Day," I reminded Jeremy.

"He said he doesn't mind that. He's happy to have the work. I also spoke to Scott, who said our cougar is mending nicely and might actually be ambulatory ahead of schedule, so I figured the sooner we got the cage ready the better."

"I agree. I'll be home late on Monday, but I'll stop in on Tuesday to look at things."

"How are you liking the great outdoors? Any more excitement?"

"Actually, yes. We've had another death."

I spent the next fifteen minutes catching Jeremy up, then took Charlie out before heading to the communal bathroom and washing the rest of the sleep from my eyes. I was walking back from the bathroom when I ran into Gordy, who was on his way to the men's bathroom.

"I can see you're on a mission, but can I ask you a quick question?"

Gordy stopped walking. "Sure. What's up?"

"I understand that although you weren't working at the camp six years ago you were in Duck Lake."

"Yes. That's true."

"When I asked you about the first woman who died, Sarah Collins, you acted as if you didn't know her."

"I didn't. You don't still suspect me of all those deaths, do you?"

"I'm not sure," I admitted. "I found an interview Gina gave to the newspaper publisher at the time, and she said you and Sarah were involved."

Gordy laughed. "Yeah, well, the bitch was lying. If you must know, I was sleeping with Gina that summer. It wasn't anything exclusive. She caught me with another woman and was quite outspoken about the fact that she was also sleeping with some guy named Quinten." Gordy shook his head. "I bet the tramp was trying to set me up. Damn. I should have known."

"Gina paired you with each of the four women who died," I informed Gordy.

"Well, the only one I was with was Cleo. Gina acted like my cheating was no big thing, but now I'm beginning to wonder. She's really good-looking and a vixen in the sack, but she has a temper that it's best not to find yourself on the wrong end of."

I narrowed my eyes. "If you had an affair with Gina six years ago and it didn't end well, why did you start working at the camp two years later?"

Gordy shrugged. "The pay and the work at the camp is the best in the area. And four years ago Gina was just another counselor, not the director. After I started working here she seemed fine. Even cool with my coming on board. I did notice her glaring at me a few times when I was with Cleo, but she never said anything." An odd look came across Gordy's face. "You don't think Gina hurt Cleo, do you?"

"I don't know. Do you?"

Gordy bit down on his lip. "God, I hope not." It appeared as if he were thinking things over. "Naw, it can't have been her. I wasn't with Wilma or Susan, so it couldn't have been a jealousy thing."

I wasn't as certain as Gordy, but I didn't have anything against Gina, so I said good-bye to Gordy and headed back to the cabin.

※※※※※※

By the time Zak joined me there I'd changed into warmer clothes in anticipation of the evening activities. The first thing on the agenda was dinner, which would be cooked in the newly reopened kitchen and fed to the kids in the large dining area. Zak had volunteered us to help serve and fortunately, I was feeling refreshed and happy to help after my nap.

As I served the hundred or so kids and staff, I couldn't help but notice that despite the deaths of two people in the past three days the atmosphere was one of joy and excitement. I guess I could understand why the kids wouldn't be all that affected. Most of them didn't know either Susan or Mrs. Potter, but even the adults were laughing and chatting as if nothing out of the ordinary had happened.

"Who is that talking to Alex?" Zak whispered from his post beside me.

I looked across the room. "You mean the boy in the blue T-shirt?"

"Yeah. The one who keeps touching her arm when he talks."

"I'm not sure," I responded. "He's not one of the kids from Ashton Falls, so he must have come from one of the other schools."

"I think I may need to go over and break things up."

"Why ever would you do that? It looks like Alex is enjoying her conversation."

"The boy is much too handsy for my taste. Besides, Alex shouldn't be talking to strangers."

I chuckled. "Zak, the kid is in sixth grade. I don't think her talking to him in the middle of a crowded cafeteria is posing much of a problem." As soon as Alex had shown an interest in boys, Zak had turned into an overprotective dad who saw any boy she spoke to as a potential threat. I hoped he mellowed out by the time Catherine was old enough to notice boys. There was no telling what he'd do to a boy who dared to talk to a daughter who shared his blood.

"It's not the discussion in the cafeteria I'm worried about. It's the one in the woods he's currently laying the groundwork for that worries me."

"Zak, the kid is twelve. Maybe thirteen. I doubt there's any big plot afoot."

Zak looked at me. "Trust me, twelve or thirteen is plenty old enough to want to get a pretty girl into the woods."

I supposed Zak had a point, but I trusted Alex implicitly. "Okay, so we'll keep an eye on the situation. Alex probably plans to hang out with her friends at the campfire like she did last night."

Zak didn't answer, but he kept his eye on the boy, who I really hoped knew Alex's fun and playful father could be a real bear when it came to protecting his little girl.

"Fred just came in to change out the trash bags," I informed Zak. "I'm going to wander over to see if I can strike up a conversation with him. Watch my station."

"Okay, but be careful. Remember, we decided to lay low so as not to arouse suspicion that we're looking in to the deaths."

"Don't worry. I know how to play it cool." I picked up an empty disposable pan and headed in the janitor's direction.

"Evening, Fred, I have another empty for you." I held up the empty container.

"No need to bring it to me. I would have come for it."

"I know. I guess I just needed a quick break and bringing you the pan was my excuse to get away for a minute. It does get noisy in here. I've only been here for a little while and I'm already hoping not to be assigned cafeteria duty again. I don't know how those of you who are here all summer do it."

Fred shrugged. "You get used to the noise after a while. After thirteen years I hardly notice it."

"You've been working here thirteen years?"

Fred moved on to the next garbage can but continued talking. "Yes, ma'am, and I'll probably be here thirteen more."

"You must really love this place."

"Yup. That I do. Don't always love everyone who comes through, but the lake and the forest feel like home."

"If you've been here thirteen years you must have known Mrs. Potter well."

Fred bowed his head. "That I did. Betty was a fine woman. Can't for the life of me figure out who would want to hurt her. Betty and me, along with Gina, have been here for a whole lotta summers. We were like a family, the three of us. It's a damn shame we lost someone so special to all of us."

"I'm very sorry for your loss," I offered. "I tried to save her, but it was too late by the time I got to her."

"It's odd about her being in the pantry and blocking the door the way she did." Fred leaned in close and lowered his voice. "I overheard the police saying you were a suspect because the killer wouldn't have been able to get back out through the door the way the body fell."

"I didn't kill Mrs. Potter. She was already almost gone when I found her."

"Figured. I've been watching you and that husband of yours. I spoke to Seth about you as well, and he said you're good folks. But I suppose the killer was a tiny thing like you and squeezed out through the door the same way you squeezed in."

I paused, then said, "I just assumed the killer went out the window."

"I don't think so. I understand the police didn't find any evidence that the killer went out the window, but they did find blood on the pantry door. The killer tried to wipe it away, but the cops, they have a way of finding the residue that's left behind."

Now this was interesting. If someone stabbed another person in the chest with enough force to kill them, it stood to reason they'd get blood on their hands. The fact that Mrs. Potter had fallen in front of the door had led me to believe whoever had killed her had gone out the window, but there was no blood from the killer's hands or clothes on the frame. If the killer could squeeze back out the door after Mrs. Potter fell in front of it, they'd have had to have been small like me, which narrowed the suspect pool significantly.

"Have you heard whether the police have any suspects?"

"Got the feeling they had one or two, but they weren't saying who they might be."

"I guess I should get back," I said after a moment. "It was nice talking to you, and if we don't have the opportunity to chat again, enjoy your summer."

"Thanks; I'll do that."

I returned to Zak long enough to let him know I was going to step outside to try to call Deputy Swanson. My conversation with Fred had not only ignited my imagination but it had reminded me about the apron I'd found in the lake. I was anxious to find out what, if any, evidence the garment had provided.

"Mrs. Zimmerman, I was just about to call you," Detective Swanson greeted me when he came on the line.

"You were? Why?"

"I got a call from Dr. Cook, informing me that you were asking about looking at the ME reports for Betty Potter and Susan Kellogg."

"Yes, I did ask, but he explained he couldn't share information regarding an active case. I can respect that, although I'd like to help in any way I can. I called you to ask about the apron we found in the lake. I hoped it would have the killer's DNA."

"Unfortunately, the only DNA on it was Mrs. Potter's. Anything else that may have been on the apron—hair or clothing fibers—had washed away. There was one interesting thing, though."

"Oh? What was that?"

"The apron had blood on it, but there were no holes in it."

I paused. "No holes? You mean Mrs. Potter wasn't wearing it when she was stabbed?"

"That's exactly what I'm saying."

"I just spoke to the janitor, who said he thought the killer squeezed back out through the door. And he said there'd been an attempt by the killer to wipe away bloody handprints from the door. I bet the killer used the apron to wipe up the blood."

"Perhaps."

"Although in a way that doesn't make sense because there were dish towels on a shelf in the pantry. I used some to try to stop Mrs. Potter's bleeding. If I was the killer and wanted to wipe away my own bloody handprints, it seems like I would have used a towel, not an apron."

"I agree with that as well."

"Unless," I added, "the killer didn't notice the blood until after they squeezed back through the door, so they grabbed whatever they found on the kitchen side of the door to clean up the mess. I don't suppose you can make out any detail on the bloodstain left on the apron, like a handprint?"

"No. Most of the blood had been washed away, but we'll keep looking. By the way, have you heard from your husband's assistant about the 911 recording?"

"Not yet. I'll have Zak call him and then Zak will call you. Pi should be home by now, and if there's anyone in the world other than Zak who can clear up the static, it's Pi."

Chapter 10

Zak called Pi, who'd just gotten home and hadn't yet had a chance to work on the tape. He'd had a long day and thought removing the static could be a lengthy process, so he didn't think he'd have news until the following day. Removing the static didn't guarantee the part of the message that was missing would come through. He wouldn't know until he was able to work with the material what would be salvageable.

I was glad Pi had decided to come home for the summer. He hadn't chosen to come to Ashton Falls last year, and I'd found I really missed him. Zak saw Pi often because they worked together and met to discuss the software projects they were working on, but it had been quite a while since I'd had the chance to visit with the young man I looked at as an oldest son.

Of course, with Levi, Ellie, and Eli living with us for the summer things were going to be crowded, but living in close quarters with people you loved was the best kind of crowded there was.

Zak let Detective Swanson know there wouldn't be news about the 911 call until the following day. Then I filled him in on my conversation with Fred. We both agreed if the killer had squeezed out through the blocked doorway, they'd have had to be thin and not broad-shouldered, leaving a suspect list that included Gina, Polly, and possibly Felix, who was much taller than me but incredibly thin.

"In terms of the dead women, it seems as if Gina and Seth are the strongest suspects. Gordy's name has come up pretty often, but I spoke to him again and I don't believe he's the killer. I also believe Polly was with him when Mrs. Potter died, and she wasn't here when the first two women died, so I think we can delete Gordy and Polly from the suspect list altogether."

"Agreed," Zak said.

"And then there's Felix. I'm not sure if he has motive to kill anyone, but his situation seems odd to me, he's been in the area for all but the first death, and he's both tall enough to have been the man we saw last night and thin enough to have squeezed through the pantry door."

"I agree we should leave him on the list, but the fact that he wasn't around for the first death leads me to suspect he isn't our guy. I did some more digging and found out he did work in finance and, as we suspected, he was accused of embezzling funds from his clients. He was in prison when the first counselor died, but I'll look for him tonight just in case he knows something. And while I haven't had the opportunity to speak to Felix, I did have a long chat with Darrell. I think we can take him off the suspect list for any of the murders. He confirmed that Gina was away from the camp on the day Wilma fell from the horse. According to him, Wilma asked to be assigned to the horseback ride that day and had discussed it with Gina before she left to take a few personal days."

"If Wilma wasn't comfortable on horseback why would she want to be assigned to that activity?"

"According to Darrell, Wilma shared with him that the other counselors had been giving her a hard time about her fear of horses. She realized little kids rode the tame horses and her fear was irrational, so she'd decided to take matters into her own hands and learn to ride. If Darrell is correct, while Wilma was with the group she wasn't the counselor in charge. Another counselor, Abby Portman, was."

I supposed that changed things a bit. If Wilma voluntarily signed up for the ride it eliminated Seth's role in assigning her in Gina's absence. It also provided Gina with an alibi for at least one of the murders, which, if our supposition that all four women were killed by the same person was correct, eliminated her as a suspect for the deaths of all the counselors. In my mind, however, she was still the prime suspect in Mrs. Potter's death.

"Okay so we have Gina, Seth, and Felix as suspects in Mrs. Potter's death," I summarized.

"What about Fred?"

I shook my head. "No. When I spoke to him I could tell he really cared about her. And I have no reason to believe he killed those counselors. As far as suspects in their deaths, assuming they weren't accidents and they were all killed by the same person, I guess we just have Seth."

"I know his name has come up a lot, but I just didn't get the serial killer vibe from him," Zak countered. "He was the one who told me about the deaths of the first three women in the first place. Why would he do that if he'd killed them?"

"To throw us off?"

"Off what? He didn't know we were investigating at that point. No one did. What about the man you heard speaking to the woman you think was Gina in the woods?"

I thought about it. I'd seen Darrell and Gordy with groups of kids, so I knew it wasn't them. Seth was with Zak then, and now that I'd heard Fred's voice I was pretty sure it wasn't him. The only other male at the camp at that time other than the other parent volunteer who was with Zak was Felix, but the voice hadn't sounded like him in the least.

"I don't know," I finally said. "The only male I can't eliminate is Felix, but it didn't sound like him."

Zak looked at his watch. "I doubt we'll figure this out tonight and we should get to the campfire. I told Gina we'd help out."

"I'll meet you there. I'm going to grab a bottle of water. All they had to drink last night was that really sweet punch."

Zak headed to the campfire and I went to the kitchen. I'd polished off all the bottled water Zak and I had bought from the little store in town, but I'd noticed a couple of cases in the kitchen when I'd been helping earlier. When I arrived, I found the new cook cleaning up after dinner.

"Can I help you?" she asked.

"I've come for a bottle of water. I'm afraid the punch that's served at the campfire is a bit too sweet for my taste. My name is Zoe, by the way."

"Judy," the cook said, handing me a bottle. "I understand you're the one who found Betty after she'd been stabbed."

"I was. I heard you were friends."

"We were. I tried to warn her that continuing to work at the camp after she had a falling-out with Gina was a bad idea, but she wouldn't listen. She was a stubborn woman and liked to do things her own way."

I unscrewed the cap from the water and took a sip. "Is it true Mrs. Potter and Gina were involved in a lawsuit over some recipes?"

Judy nodded. "Not sure it would have gone anywhere, but Betty was madder than a cat with its tail stuck in the screen door when she found her recipes in Gina's cookbook. Gina argued that they were developed for use at the camp, so the camp owned them and, as administrator, she had the right to use them, but Betty didn't see it that way."

"Who actually owns the camp?"

"The property is owned by one of the local families who lease it to a nonprofit that was set up to provide the camp experience to kids in the area. The nonprofit is overseen by a board of directors who hire an administrator to run things. Gina took over three or maybe it was four years ago. Can't rightly remember."

"And before that she was a counselor?"

"Lead counselor."

I took another sip of my water before I continued. "And you've been subbing at the camp for a number of years?"

"Yeah. Been more than a decade, I reckon. Never wanted a full-time gig, but filling in now and then provides me with some spending money."

"So you aren't going to stay on full time now that Mrs. Potter is gone?"

"No. Gina said there'd be a new cook starting on Tuesday of next week, so I'm just here until then. Almost didn't want to do that after what happened with Betty, but Gina offered me a sizable salary for just a few days' work, so I took a chance, hoping Betty's killer didn't have a beef with me."

"Any idea who the killer might be?"

"I've got a few ideas, but I figure it wouldn't be in my best interests to say. You never know who might be listening. Now I best get back to work. Got kids of my own to feed. It was nice meeting you."

"It was nice meeting you too." I held up my bottle. "And thanks for the water."

I headed toward the campfire, wondering if Zak had managed to pull Felix aside, although I really couldn't see why he'd kill Mrs. Potter. I did think it would be worth our while to speak to him, but my Zodar told me he wasn't our guy. I was halfway there when my phone rang.

"Hey, Pi. Are you all settled in?"

"Getting there. Listen, I was trying to reach Zak, but he isn't picking up."

"He's at the campfire, which can be very noisy. He may not have heard his phone ring. I'm heading in that direction. I can have him call you or I can give him a message."

"Just tell him I was able to clean up the 911 call quicker than I expected. There are still a few words I can't make out, but the woman who called basically gave the operator her name and location and then said the dirty skunk who stole her recipes was trying to attack her and had her trapped in the pantry. After that the call cuts out, but then she says something about a serial killer, a dirty cap, and ritual beads. After that there was the sound of a struggle and the phone went dead.

Gina. The killer had to be Gina. Detective Swanson had thought Mrs. Potter had said *cereal* and *beans*, but what she'd really said was *serial* and *beads*.

"Thanks, Pi. I'm going to call the detective right now. I'll have Zak get back to you when he gets a chance."

I called Detective Swanson, but he didn't pick up, so I called the police station. Luckily, Officer Michaelson was still there, so I passed on what Pi had told me. He told me to wait for him near the front entrance of the camp and not to tell anyone else what I'd learned until he arrived because he didn't want Gina being tipped off before he could get there. I agreed and headed to the front gate. I tried calling Zak, but he didn't pick up this time either, so I left a message letting him know what I was doing and asking him to meet me at the gate if he could get away.

I settled in, expecting to wait at least fifteen minutes, but after only a couple of minutes Officer Michaelson pulled up in a red truck.

"That was fast," I said. Michaelson was dressed casually in jeans and a T-shirt rather than his police uniform.

"I had the phone at the station forwarded to my cell and was on my way out to join the campfire when you called."

"Oh. Well, I guess that was convenient. I'm pretty sure Gina is there. Should I tell her you're here to speak to her or should we wait for backup?"

"Whoa. Let's slow down a bit, little darlin'. I've found that when handling these situations timing is key. I think the two of us should have a little chat to get our ducks in a row."

Ducks in a row? Oh God. I suddenly realized the man Gina had been talking to in the woods was Officer Michaelson. I should have recognized his voice, but never in a million years would I think he'd be the killer I was now certain was working with Gina. I swallowed hard and tried not to let my expression give away the fact that I was suddenly terrified.

Serial killer, dirty cap, and *ritual beads...*

Dirty cap must have been dirty *cop*. I glanced at Michaelson's face and noticed the beaded necklace around his throat. The beads were pure black with one white one in the center, exactly like the ones the women who'd died had worn when they'd had their accidents.

"Okay," I said as calmly as I could manage, "I guess that makes sense. What do we need to figure out?"

"The tape you claim to have of Mrs. Potter's 911 call. Do you have it on you?"

"No. It was sent to an associate of my husband. He called me with the results of his effort just before I called the police station."

Officer Michaelson frowned. "I see. That does provide a bit of a problem."

"Oh? And why is that?"

"No need to worry your pretty head about it. So, on the tape, did Betty mention her attacker by name?"

"No. But it seemed clear it was Gina, so should we go arrest her?"

"Did you tell anyone else what was on the tape?"

"I left the details on Detective Swanson's cell."

Officer Michaelson's lips tightened. "I see. Guess I should have taken Gina's advice and taken care of you first thing instead of waiting."

"It was you," I accused now that I realized I wasn't going to get out of this without a struggle. "You killed those women. Why?"

Michaelson rubbed the beads around his neck with his left hand, "Just scratching an itch."

I felt the familiar nausea returning. "Mrs. Potter found out somehow. She threatened to go to the police, so you killed her."

"That lady should have minded her own business and she wouldn't have had to die. When Betty told Gina what she'd figured out, Gina took care of her. That would have been the end of it, but you started nosing around."

I could feel my heart pounding in my chest. I had an overwhelming urge to run, which was most likely what Susan had been doing when she fell off the ledge, but I forced myself to keep my head. "So what now? Are you going to kill me too?"

"I guess I'm going to have to." He pulled a gun out of his waistband. He pointed it at me and told me to get into his truck. I figured if I did that Catherine and I were both dead, so I did the only thing I could think of: threw up on his shoe. That distracted him long enough for me to kick him in the groin. I knew that wouldn't slow him down for long, so I took off running as fast as I could with the few seconds' head start my actions had bought me.

It didn't take long before I heard the sound of a gun being fired and a bullet whizzing past my head. I'd run away from the camp because I hadn't wanted any of the kids to get caught in the crossfire, but all I had ahead of me was an endless expanse of deserted road surrounded on both sides by dense forest. My only hope was to find a place to hide until help arrived. I remembered that the river ran parallel to the road on the other side, so I darted across the road with the idea of following it when a car came from around the corner and knocked me onto the embankment.

"Mrs. Zimmerman," Detective Swanson said as he knelt next to me. "Are you okay?"

I put my hand on my stomach as tears streamed down my face. *Please God, let Catherine be okay.* "I don't know. The fall knocked the wind out of me, but you really weren't going very fast." I tried to sit up, but my head was throbbing. I took several deep breaths, then sat up the rest of the way. "The killer is Officer Michaelson. He was chasing me. He has a gun."

Detective Swanson helped me to my feet and then into his car. "Wait here. I'll be right back."

I watched as he disappeared into the trees. Several seconds later, I heard three gunshots fired in rapid succession. I waited with tears streaming down my face to find out which man had shot the other and whether Catherine and I would live to see another day.

After several minutes of living in complete terror Detective Swanson returned to the car. He informed me that Michaelson was wounded, Gina had been detained by Seth, who was holding her until backup arrived, and an ambulance was on the way.

"Zak?" I asked.

"On his way. He can ride with you in the ambulance. I'll meet you after I get things buttoned up here."

I nodded because I was crying too hard to speak. I knew my injuries were minor; what I didn't know was how well Catherine had survived the ordeal.

Zak arrived at the car at about the same time the ambulance showed up. I was loaded onto a gurney while Zak clung to my hand like he'd never let go.

"It's going to be okay," Zak said with tears running down his own face.

"The baby..."

Zak put his hand on my stomach. "This little one is a Donovan. I have a feeling she's going to be as tough as her mother."

I put my hand over the one Zak still had on my stomach and prayed harder than I ever had in my life.

Chapter 11

Monday, May 29

I can't begin to express how very happy and grateful I was to be home for Memorial Day, BBQing steaks with my family and friends. I'd spent two days in the hospital just to be extra sure Catherine was okay, then Zak had brought me home yesterday in the late afternoon and made me sleep for twelve hours before deciding I really was fine and perfectly capable of spending time with those I loved most.

"Mama says you have a baby in your tummy," my three-year-old sister Harper said after climbing into my lap.

"I do have a baby in my tummy," I confirmed. "What do you think about that?"

Harper's bright blue eyes grew serious as she pondered my question. "Can I play with her?"

"When she gets old enough."

"Can I hold her?"

"Yes." I wrapped Harper in a tight hug. "You can hold her all you want as long as there's an adult there to supervise."

Harper dipped her cap of dark curls as she looked down at my lap. "I don't see a baby."

"It's too soon to see her yet, but in a few months, we'll be able to feel her kick."

"Mama said it's not nice to kick people."

I laughed. "Mama's right, but in the case of a baby in your tummy I imagine feeling her kick for the first time is pretty wonderful."

Harper bit her lip as she patted my stomach with her hand. I could almost see her little mind working a mile a minute. "Is your baby going to be my sister?"

"No, you're going to be her aunt and she'll be your niece."

Harper frowned. "I'm not an ant."

"Not the creepy-crawly kind of ant; the kind of aunt your friend Celeste has."

Harper looked confused and I guess I didn't blame her. Having an aunt was a difficult enough concept for a three-year-old but being an aunt when you were only three must not make any sense at all.

Harper sat quietly as she continued to ponder the situation until Jeremy's daughter, Morgan Rose, who was the same age as Harper, wandered over and climbed onto my lap along with her best friend.

"Zoe has a baby in her tummy," Harper informed her friend.

"Is it a puppy like Flower has?"

"Is it?" Harper turned and looked at me with a huge grin on her face.

"No. It's a human baby."

Harper looked disappointed by that.

"So you named your new dog Flower?" I asked Morgan.

"Rosalie named her Sadie, but I like flowers. Daddy said she has puppies in her tummy."

"Maybe one is pink," Harper squealed.

I sat with the two little girls in my lap listening to their banter and longing for the day I'd be holding Eli and Catherine while they planned an adventure only three-year-olds can plan. The past few days had been tough on me both physically and mentally. Officer Michaelson had eventually confessed to Detective Swanson that not only had he killed all four of the counselors but he'd slept with three of them beforehand. He'd seduced them, then led them into the woods, where he'd had sex with them, given them each a bracelet, then killed them in such a way that it looked like an accident. Wilma was the only one who wouldn't play along, but he'd already developed an itch that needed scratching when he met her, so he'd talked her into learning to ride and then got her horse to bolt with a well-placed rock delivered via slingshot. After he'd responded to the call on his police radio he'd slipped the bracelet onto her wrist. While not as satisfying as the others, it completed the ritual, allowing his obsession to rest until the next time.

As it turned out, though Michaelson had done the killing, Gina was part of the fantasy. The two were in a strange relationship, identifying and killing the women as some sort of sex play. When Gina found out Mrs. Potter had somehow figured out what was going on, she'd killed her. She suspected Susan may have seen something, so she had Michaelson take care of her as well, even though her death hadn't fit the pattern of waiting until the end of camp while the anticipation of what they would do had time to intensify.

I hated to ruin this perfect day with thoughts of murder, so I was relieved when Alex came in my direction after Zak whispered something in her ear.

"Zak said he doesn't want you to get tired out. He wants me to take Harper and Morgan outside."

"I'm fine, but I do think the girls would enjoy playing on the beach for a while. Do you mind watching them?"

"No, I don't mind." Alex held out her hands. "Come on, girls. Let's build a sandcastle."

The girls squealed in delight. Alex had quite a way with the little ones. Eli adored her already and I was certain Catherine would as well.

"How are you feeling?" Ellie sat down next to me after Alex had led the girls away.

"I'm feeling fine. The doctor said I was fine. I wish everyone would stop worrying."

"You were hit by a car," Ellie reminded me. "It's only by the grace of God that you and Catherine are fine. Let the people who love you fuss over you a little."

I laid my head on Ellie's shoulder. "Okay. You're right. Fuss all you want."

Ellie clasped my hand with hers. "I'm afraid I won't have long before Eli wakes up from his nap, but I wanted to take a minute to make sure you really are okay and not just being Zoe."

I lifted my head from Ellie's shoulder. "What does that mean?"

"It means you never want to appear vulnerable and you always try to put on a brave face and act like everything is fine even when it isn't."

I squeezed Ellie's hand. "In this case I really am okay. I will say it may be a very long time before I want to go camping again, though."

"I hear ya. Levi actually suggested a camping trip this summer. I reminded him that we have a newborn, but he insists a little dirt under the fingernails is good for babies. Personally, I'm happy to wait to introduce Eli to camping until after he can walk."

"Then you'll be paranoid about him toddling too close to the fire or wandering off."

"Good point. We'll wait until he's Scooter's age. Where is Scooter anyway? I haven't seen him all day."

"He's out on the boat with Pi and Tucker. They'll be back in time for dinner."

"I bet Scooter is happy to have his honorary big brother home for the summer."

"Thrilled."

Ellie looked up toward the stairs. "Sounds like someone's awake. Duty calls."

I watched Ellie as she walked to the stairs. I'd been sitting right next to Ellie and hadn't heard Eli cry. I hoped I wasn't going to be a defective mother. I worried about that a lot more than I cared to admit.

The thing about having a large family was that when one person walked away there was always someone else to take their place. It wasn't even a minute before my dad came over and sat down in Ellie's place next to me.

"It seems congratulations are in order."

I hugged my dad. "I'm sorry I didn't tell you sooner. I just needed time."

"It's fine, sweetheart. I understand. How are you feeling?"

"I'm fine. Things got pretty scary for a while, but the doctor said the baby's fine and I know in my heart she is."

"*She*?"

"Mother's intuition." I decided to leave out the part about the ghost. "Harper is disappointed I'm not having puppies, though."

Dad laughed. "She's been asking for one. We already have four dogs, but I know how much kids love puppies. Maybe I'll get her one for Christmas."

"Something small that will stay small and she can carry around. Or maybe even a kitten. I seem to remember having a kitten when I was around her age. It slept with me and let me hold it, but it was a lot easier to take care of than a puppy."

"Good idea. I'll talk to your mom about it. If I can get a word in edgewise with all the planning going on."

"Planning?" I asked.

"She's planning a baby shower."

I groaned. I was afraid this was going to be my wedding all over again. Zak's mom had already announced her plans to spend the entire month the baby was due with us. She insisted I'd need help. I was afraid help wouldn't be the only thing she'd be bringing.

"Is it too late to head into the woods and have my baby there?"

Dad patted my leg. "'Fraid so. The women in your life have already organized every little detail so you won't have to worry about a thing."

"Fantastic," I groaned. "That's just what I need."

"Guess I should head outside and help Grandpa get the grill ready." Dad leaned over and kissed me on the cheek. "I really am happy for you."

"Thanks, Dad."

The chair next to me didn't fill with another concerned loved one immediately, so I took advantage of the lull and headed outside. Charlie saw me leave the house and followed behind me. I headed down the narrow path that connected the house with the boathouse I owned but Levi and Ellie lived in when it wasn't being renovated. When I arrived at the structure that was still in the beginning stages of the remodel I noticed Levi standing in front of the house and frowning at something.

"Problem?" I asked.

He turned, seemingly surprised to find me standing there. "I'm wondering if we should add a second story as long as we're doing this."

"Second story?" I asked. The boathouse originally had consisted of a small living area, a small kitchen, a bathroom, and a loft I'd used as a bedroom. When I moved in with Zak, Ellie moved into the boathouse, and when Ellie and Levi married he moved in as well. Zak and I thought it would be too small once Baby Eli was born, but we liked having our best friends just down the beach, so we'd decided to add on a large master suite, a second bedroom, and a much larger kitchen.

"Ellie and I have discussed having three children, two boys and a girl. The extra room with this remodel will be perfect for Ellie, Eli, and me, but once we have another baby I'm afraid it will already be too small. I figured a second story divided into three bedrooms and a bath for the kids would serve us for a lifetime."

I couldn't help but smile. Here Levi was, talking about three kids after insisting for most of his life that the perfect number of children was zero. "I think a second story is a perfect idea. It's early in the remodel, so it might not be too late. I'll talk to Zak about it after everyone goes home."

Levi hugged me. "Thanks, Zoe. I really want our kids to grow up living next door to one another. Having friends like you and Ellie when I was growing up made all the difference to me."

I slipped my arm around Levi's waist as we stood looking at the boathouse. "Yeah, we were quite the dynamic trio."

******

"That turned out to be very nice," Zak said that night after everyone had left, the kids had gone to their rooms, and Levi, Ellie, and Eli had retired to their suite.

"It really was," I purred with delight as I leaned back in my lounge chair and looked at the stars while Zak rubbed my feet. He'd read that it was important to rub the feet of expectant mothers to offset the effect of supporting extra weight, although so far, I hadn't gained a pound, but I wasn't going to point that out. "I took a short walk today and ran into Levi at the boathouse. He suggested adding a second story with three extra bedrooms and an extra bath as long as we're having everything torn up anyway. It seems he and Ellie plan to have three children, two boys and a girl, and he wanted to be sure they'd grow up next door to our kids, who he's certain will be their best friends."

"I suppose a second story is a good idea. I guess I should have thought of it. I'll call the architect tomorrow. They've been doing the prep and groundwork but haven't actually started the structure yet, so it should be doable."

I closed my eyes and the fatigue I'd been fighting the past few hours began to set in. "I'm glad. I love the idea of our kids and Levi and Ellie's having one another's backs like Levi and Ellie always had mine."

"Have you thought about how many kids you want?" Zak asked.

"I guess I haven't. Have you?"

"How about five?"

My eyes popped open. "Five?"

"We have a big enough house."

"There's no law that says we have to fill all the rooms. Besides, we have Scooter and Alex already, and Pi pops in and out so we have to keep a room for him. How about three?"

Zak smiled. "Two girls and a boy?"

I laced my fingers through Zak's. "Unlike Levi, I don't have the need to define gender at this point. How about for now we just say Catherine and whoever else God decides to bless us with."

Zak stretched out on the lounge chair next to me, wrapping me in his arms, though he didn't speak. The pump from the pool clicked on, providing a pleasant hum. I tried to look up at the stars but eventually fell asleep. At some point between drifting off on the lounge and waking in my own bed, I dreamed of three

little Zimmermans and three little
Dentons, all playing together and sharing
dreams for the future, as best friends do.

Recipes

Tomato Cucumber Salad—submitted by Sharon Lynne
Broiled Shrimp—submitted by Nancy Farris
Caramel Brownies—submitted by Pam Curran
Grandma's Old-Fashioned Ice Cream Toppings—submitted by Vivian Shane

Tomato Cucumber Salad

Submitted by Sharon Lynne

2 nice red tomatoes, chopped in bite-size pieces
1 cucumber, peeled and cut in half, then sliced
¼ small red onion, peeled and sliced, or to taste

Simple balsamic vinaigrette:
¾ cup extra-virgin olive oil
¼ cup balsamic vinegar
Salt
Freshly ground black pepper
Minced garlic, fresh or dried herbs, 1 tsp.
Dijon mustard (optional)

Combine salad ingredients in a small bowl.

For the vinaigrette:

Combine the olive oil and balsamic in a jar or other container with a good-sealing lid. Add a big pinch of salt and a few grinds of black pepper. Screw on the lid and shake vigorously. Dip a piece of lettuce into the vinaigrette and taste. Adjust the salt, pepper, or the proportion of oil and vinegar to taste.

Broiled Shrimp

Submitted by Nancy Farris

One of our favorite weeknight meals. It's really good and really easy and quick!

1 lb. large shrimp, peeled and deveined
12 large pimento-stuffed olives, quartered lengthwise
8 oz. cherry or grape tomatoes, cut in half lengthwise
2 cloves garlic, minced
1 tbs. thyme, fresh or dried
1 tsp. salt
1 lemon, juiced
4 tbs. olive oil

Preheat broiler.

Put all ingredients into large bowl and toss thoroughly. Place in large, ovenproof baking dish. Place under broiler for 5 minutes. Remove and stir so that any uncooked shrimp will be exposed. Place back under broiler for another 3–4 minutes until shrimp is cooked.

Serve in the baking dish with a loaf of crusty bread for dipping.

Serves 2

Caramel Brownies

Submitted by Pam Curran

1 pkg. Kraft caramels
⅔ cup evaporated milk
2 sticks margarine
1 box German chocolate cake mix
1 cup milk chocolate chips

Melt caramels and ⅓ cup evaporated milk over double boiler and set aside. Melt margarine. Mix cake mix, ⅓ cup evaporated milk, and margarine. Press ½ cake mixture in bottom of a 9 x 13 cake pan. Bake for 6 minutes at 350 degrees. Sprinkle with milk chocolate chips. If desired, add 1 cup chopped pecans at this time. Drizzle melted caramel over top of mixture. Sprinkle remaining cake mixture over top. Bake at 350 degrees for 18–20 minutes. Allow to cool, then cut into bars.

Grandma's Old-Fashioned Ice Cream Toppings

Submitted by Vivian Shane

We do love our ice cream in my house! Here are two of our favorite toppings; they taste so much better than store-bought toppings and don't take very much effort.

Old-Fashioned Hot Fudge Sauce
Melt 1 cup chocolate chips and ½ cup butter in a heavy-bottomed pan. Add 2 cups powdered sugar and 1½ cups evaporated milk. Cook until thick and smooth. Add ½ tsp. vanilla, stir, and it's ready for ice cream!

Old-Fashioned Caramel Sauce
1 cup brown sugar
1 tbs. cornstarch
1 cup heavy cream
2 tbs. apple cider
1 tbs. butter

Mix all ingredients together in a heavy-bottomed pan and place over low heat. Stir frequently as it thickens to a rich, golden brown. Remove from heat and serve warm over ice cream (this also tastes great over apple crisp).

Books by Kathi Daley

Come for the murder, stay for the romance.

Zoe Donovan Cozy Mystery:

Halloween Hijinks
The Trouble With Turkeys
Christmas Crazy
Cupid's Curse
Big Bunny Bump-off
Beach Blanket Barbie
Maui Madness
Derby Divas
Haunted Hamlet
Turkeys, Tuxes, and Tabbies
Christmas Cozy
Alaskan Alliance
Matrimony Meltdown
Soul Surrender
Heavenly Honeymoon
Hopscotch Homicide
Ghostly Graveyard
Santa Sleuth
Shamrock Shenanigans
Kitten Kaboodle
Costume Catastrophe
Candy Cane Caper
Holiday Hangover

Easter Escapade
Camp Carter
Trick or Treason – *September 2017*
Reindeer Roundup – *December 2017*

Zimmerman Academy The New Normal
Ashton Falls Cozy Cookbook

Tj Jensen Paradise Lake Mysteries by Henery Press

Pumpkins in Paradise
Snowmen in Paradise
Bikinis in Paradise
Christmas in Paradise
Puppies in Paradise
Halloween in Paradise
Treasure in Paradise
Fireworks in Paradise – *October 2017*

Whales and Tails Cozy Mystery:

Romeow and Juliet
The Mad Catter
Grimm's Furry Tail
Much Ado About Felines
Legend of Tabby Hollow
Cat of Christmas Past
A Tale of Two Tabbies
The Great Catsby
Count Catula
The Cat of Christmas Present
A Winter's Tail
Taming of the Tabby
Frankencat – *August 2017*
The Cat of Christmas Futuure – November 2017
The Cat of New Orleans – *February 2018*

Seacliff High Mystery:

The Secret
The Curse
The Relic
The Conspiracy
The Grudge
The Shadow
The Haunting – *September 2017*

Sand and Sea Hawaiian Mystery:
Murder at Dolphin Bay
Murder at Sunrise Beach
Murder at the Witching Hour
Murder at Christmas
Murder at Turtle Cove
Murder at Water's Edge
Murder at Midnight – *October 2017*

Road to Christmas Romance:
Road to Christmas Past

Writer's Retreat Southern Mystery:
First Case
Second Look
Third Strike – *August 2017*
Fourth Victim – *October 2017*

USA Today Bestselling Author Kathi Daley lives with her husband Ken in beautiful Lake Tahoe. When she isn't writing, she likes to read (preferably at the beach or by the fire), cook (preferably something with chocolate or cheese), and garden (planting and planning, not weeding). She also enjoys spending time on the water when she's not hiking, biking, or snowshoeing the miles of desolate trails surrounding her home.

Kathi uses the mountain setting in which she lives, along with the animals (wild and domestic) that share her home, as inspiration for her cozy mysteries.

Kathi is a top 100 mystery writer for Amazon and won the 2014 award for both Best Cozy Mystery Author and Best Cozy Mystery Series.

She currently writes six series: Zoe Donovan Cozy Mysteries, Whales and Tails Island Mysteries, Sand and Sea Hawaiian Mysteries, Writer's Retreat Southern Mysteries, Tj Jensen Paradise Lake Mysteries, and Seacliff High Teen Mysteries.

Giveaway:

I do a giveaway for books, swag, and gift cards every week in my newsletter, *The Daley Weekly* **http://eepurl.com/NRPDf**

Other links to check out:
Kathi Daley Blog – publishes each Friday **http://kathidaleyblog.com**
Webpage – **www.kathidaley.com**
Facebook at Kathi Daley Books – **www.facebook.com/kathidaleybooks**
Kathi Daley Books Group Page – **https://www.facebook.com/groups/569578823146850/**
E-mail – **kathidaley@kathidaley.com**
Goodreads – **https://www.goodreads.com/author/show/7278377.Kathi_Daley**
Twitter at Kathi Daley@kathidaley – **https://twitter.com/kathidaley**
Amazon Author Page – **https://www.amazon.com/author/kathidaley**
BookBub – **https://www.bookbub.com/authors/kathi-daley**
Pinterest – **http://www.pinterest.com/kathidaley/**

34526024R00122

Made in the USA
Lexington, KY
24 March 2019